I0760468

Forever Misplaced

Heather Michelle

Books by Heather Michelle

IN RECOMMENDED READING ORDER

The Misplaced Children Series

A Misplaced Child

A Misplaced Hope

A Misplaced Life

Novellas

Forever Misplaced (you are here)

Unseen Consequences

The Unseen Series

A Girl Unseen (Coming soon)

This is a work of fiction. Names, characters, places, and incidents either are the product of the author's imagination or are used fictitiously.

Late for Dinner Press LLC
P.O. Box 982
Acworth, GA 30101

Edited by Nicole Schuette: www.nicoleschuette.com

First Edition: August 2022
ISBN 978-1-952857-11-9

To Kody. You owe me now.

The Kingdom of Sixteen

"The Twoshy"

Mimor Sea
Skuna
Duum
Wedren
Scuoso
Qosha
Eplaria
Breora
Pundica
Vasniydor
Rohap
Oskela
Leronia
Ustra
Aluna
The Variant Forest
Raynor Ocean
Tokke Mountains
Backirk Ocean

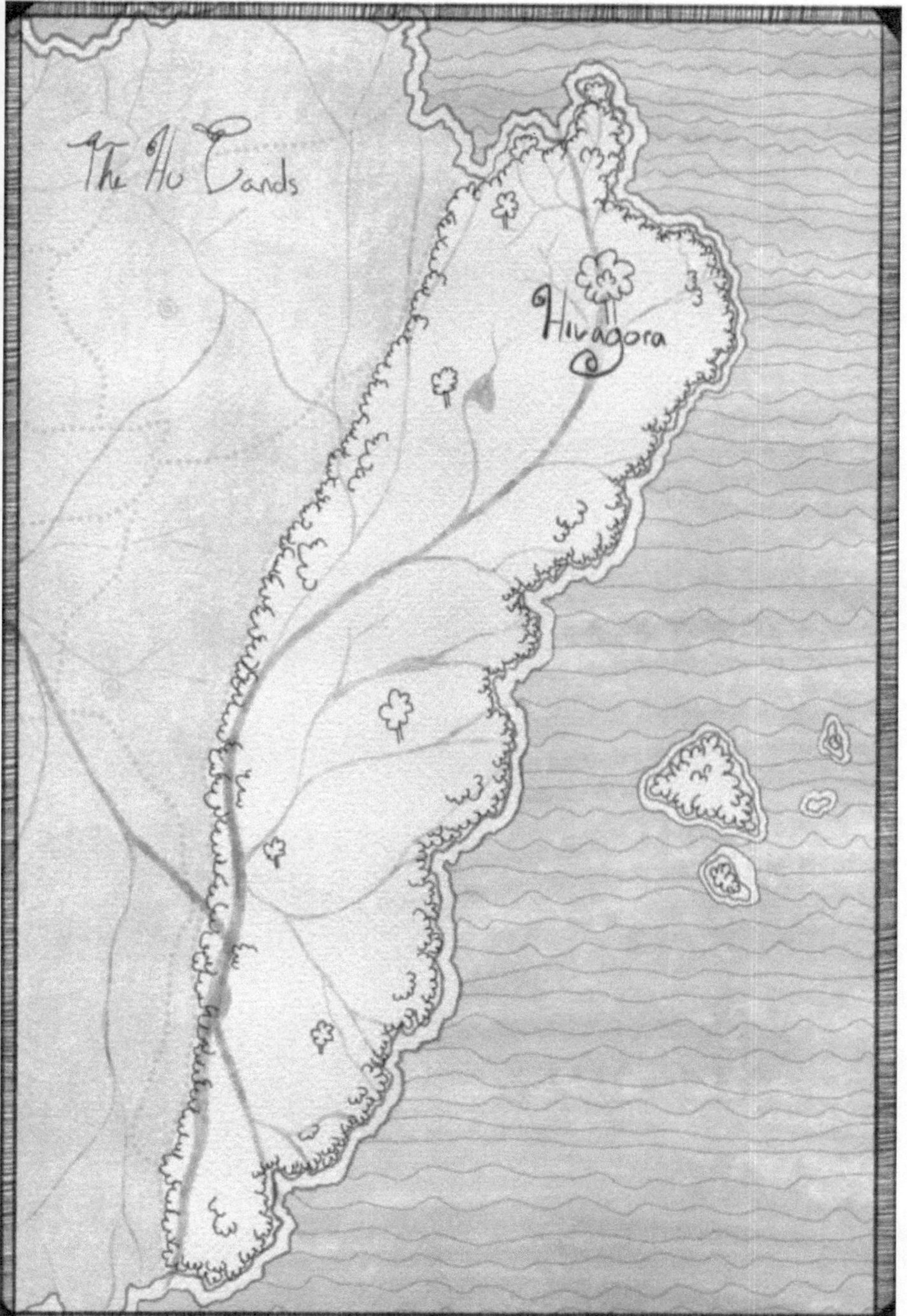
The Hu Lands
Hivagora

Forever Misplaced

A MISPLACED CHILDREN NOVELLA

HEATHER MICHELLE

Chapter One

Kody pounded on the locked door of her apartment. "Open up, Roger. This isn't funny." She jiggled the handle again, but he'd locked the top deadbolt, only accessible on the inside. The landlady called it a safety feature. Now, that safety feature was ruining her life.

Her day had been great. A quiet morning working the early shift at the bookstore and two call backs resulting in interviews on Monday, bringing her one step closer to the life she wanted. Mindlessly placing new release after new release on the shelf the remainder of the morning let her brain wander. It dawned on her with the new doors in her life opening that it was time to talk with Roger about where their relationship was going. She texted him on her break and asked if they could talk when she got home.

What an epic backfire.

She pounded on the door again, and the phone in her pocket buzzed. She pulled it out. Roger.

She accepted the call.

"Let me in, Roger. I know you're in there."

"Look, babe, you were the one who wanted to break up," he

said in the soft, serious voice he used for touchy subjects in front of someone he wanted to impress.

"I didn't want to break up," Kody hissed into the phone. "I said we needed to talk about us."

In their texts, he'd jumped to conclusions, accusing her of cheating and telling her not to come back to their apartment. They were done, he said.

She didn't get it. He was usually more even-tempered than this. A laid-back guy, so placid in the day-to-day it drove Kody mad just trying to get his opinion on something.

Was it her? Was she not enough for him?

She leaned against the door, waiting for him to answer.

"Well, what's done is done," Roger said. "I think we should go our separate ways before things get even more complicated."

"Roger, where am I supposed to go?" she asked, her heart in her voice. She wanted to build a life with him, and before now, he seemed on board. "Everything I own is in that apartment."

"I'll let you in tomorrow when you're a little less emotional. I can't just let you live in my apartment for free, babe. That's not how the real world works."

Free? What was he talking about? When had she lived there for free? Roger said they should pool their finances from day one, which had always meant she paid the bills and he sometimes made grand gestures of movie tickets or a night out.

Something in her brain snapped, like a spark igniting a fire. Her vision went red, and she kicked the door again and again.

"For free!?" She pounded the wood with her fists, rattling the small numbers nailed on the apartment door. "I've been paying the rent for the last year, you mother f—"

The apartment door to Kody's right cracked open and her elderly neighbor poked her head out. Kody grimaced and gave the old woman a nod before lifting the phone back to her ear.

"Look. I get you're upset, babe, but the apartment's in my name, remember? You didn't have the credit. But I can't keep letting you live here for nothing. You just got to move on and stand on your own for once."

The words stung.

How many homes had she moved into as a foster kid and felt like a stranger leaching off the goodness of someone else? She told Roger that once, how she was so excited to get her own place after she turned eighteen. Working her butt off for minimum wage while going to community college, then online courses to finish her degree. Yeah, she had a roommate, but rent was expensive. Then her roommate got married. She and Roger had only just started dating, but she'd known him for a while and trusted him. He suggested they get a place together, and Kody agreed. That was two years ago.

The high notes of a giggle broke through the phone speaker, and the sting of Roger's words melted against the flames of her sudden, intense anger.

"Who the hell is that? Roger! Who do you have in there? Have you been cheating on me? Is that what this is?" *He* accused *her* of cheating. Was it because of a guilty conscience?

"Babe, that's the TV. You're delusional. Look, I'm hanging up. You can come back tomorrow for your stuff. I'll have it sitting on the front porch."

"You will not touch my stuff, Roger. Let me in now or I'm calling the cops."

"Call them and tell them what? Your boyfriend won't let you into his apartment? Who do you think they're going to believe in this situation, babe? Look, I got to go. Stop by tomorrow. Your stuff will be on the porch."

The phone clicked and went dead in Kody's hand. Through the door, Roger's deep voice rumbled and a high-pitched laugh answered. She kicked the door once more in frustration, but regretted it. Roger would only think he won.

From the day she entered the system a nameless, anonymous baby, she had been taught time and time again that she could only trust herself and what she could make with her own hands. And so she fought for her independence. Every decision she made, every late night studying and twelve-hour shift, it was all to reach a place where she would never again be forced to pack a trash bag with her life's possessions and abandon another home with no notice.

She was so close. One of the interviews on Monday would finally put her degree to use and pay twice what she made at the bookstore.

At first Roger hadn't fit into her plan but building a life with someone else had sounded so good, and her heart had hoped for something brighter than cold independence. Roger proved her hope naive, but she would never again make the same mistake.

Kody sighed and left the apartment complex, setting off along a main road into town. She would head to her favorite coffee shop where she could think and use the Wi-Fi to look up cohabitation laws in their state. Her name wasn't on the lease, but it was her residence, and she had the bills and rent receipts to prove it, as long as Roger didn't do something to them before she could get in. She could crash on her college roommate's couch for the night, but she didn't want to bother her. Maybe she would put her emergency credit card to use while she secured a crappy apartment in a rough part of town. She was more established now. Someone would rent to her.

With a plan in mind, she could breathe easier. It was how she got through life—make a plan, breathe, follow the plan.

She'd been too submissive in their relationship. She spent too long enjoying the comfort of having someone to call hers and let the part of herself who always fought to get ahead fade into the background. Never again. Never again would she let some man make her feel safe and forget she was the only one looking out for herself.

The bright, end of winter sun chased off the crisp chill in the air. Green shoots popped up out of the dead earth on the sides of the road as spring threatened to emerge.

Kody glared at the patch of daffodils.

Daffodils always caused a flurry of mixed emotions within her spirit. The sight of their leaves poking up through the bracken of the winter months signaled the end of her favorite time of year. They were an omen for the death of winter, yet when she passed a horde of the bright yellow bulbs bursting above the cheery green leaves and watched their heads bob and wave in the light breeze, she couldn't help but smile. She wanted to hate these harbingers of the death of her beloved winter, but the edges of her lips bent into a smile and she found she could not do so.

Kody hated the summer. She hated to be hot and sweaty, and in the long-sleeved shirts she wore year round, the heat became unbearable.

The only way to hide pit stains in the summer was to wear black, and that only made the heat worse.

But that had been her life for well over a decade, ever since her skin issues became more apparent, and kids started making fun of her.

Her skin color, she'd known from a young age, was important to how those around her perceived her. She wasn't black, or white, or Asian, or Latina but an unguessable blend forever unknown by the absence of parents and family. Being brown wasn't the worst thing growing up. She didn't burn easily, and she quite liked her unruly curls. Brown had been nice, but when she turned ten, standing in the sun, it was hard to miss the odd discoloration of her skin. Streaks of green wound over her arms and legs, up her neck and onto her face. One foster mother wondered if maybe they were oddly hued scars, darkening with age.

Long sleeves covered most of the oddity, but that foster mother refused to let her wear foundation. The next foster home hadn't cared, or even noticed, as she lathered on makeup, causing a terrible case of acne. From there, the breakouts were enough to rationalize the need for makeup until she graduated and learned a better skincare routine.

Roger was her first boyfriend that didn't seem bothered by her discoloration. He was the first man she ever truly let her guard down with. There were other boys, the ones who made nasty comments when they got her jacket off and saw her warm brown skin marred by the faint green streaks that swirled her body. The comments always killed the friendship and then names came later. But Roger, the first and only time he saw her without her long-sleeved shirt in good lighting, said nothing. The silence was heavy, but easier to deal with than anything he could have said.

She'd been stupid to think disinterest was enough to build a relationship on.

Kody continued down the road, too frustrated to bother with the bus. She held her breath whenever a car passed and kicked up dirt and exhaust in her face. Halfway to her destination, a sixteen-wheeler passed, and she threw an arm over her face to block the dust and dirt. The dust caught the light, shimmering in the air, and the world seemed to shift around her. As if caught in a stiff vortex of air coming off the truck, the wind caught her, and Kody's heart skipped a beat as her feet fell out from under her. She fell, pulled to the left, and her eyes stared into the face of an oncoming truck just before impact.

Chapter Two

Kody landed hard on her elbow and tensed, waiting for the impact of the truck.

It didn't come.

She scrambled to her knees. The world wasn't what it had been a moment before. Gone was the sun reflecting off the asphalt. Gone were the light posts and bus stops and the general noise of running motors and speeding cars. Everything was green and slow. Trees swayed in a warm breeze and the sun filtered down through the foliage and cast a warm green glow to the earth.

Kody blinked and rubbed her eyes. Her skin buzzed, and her head swam with the sudden change in light, temperature, sound, and literally every other external factor she could think of. She took a deep breath, and it was as if she'd never done so before. There was something alive all around her, pulsing in the air and flowing below the ground.

A leaf fell from the canopy above, and Kody lazily reached out a hand but froze at what met her eyes.

Her hand glowed. Not the entire hand, but the streaks she had known to shine green in the right light were now radiating a solid green hue. She turned her hand, and the spiral running down her wrist and around her thumb continued in a glowing swirl on her palm. It had always been faint before, but now it was unmistakable.

This had to be a hallucination. She could never hide her green bits if they glowed. Was the foundation on her face even working anymore?

She pulled up her sleeves, and sure enough, the glow continued, following the path of her spirals. Lifting her sweatshirt, even her stomach spirals glowed. Her heart raced. She stuck her hands in her pockets, hoping no one was near enough to see. Peering around her curls, she gazed through the trunks of wide trees, ferns, and brambles but saw no one. She was completely alone in this secluded stretch of forest.

Living in the city, Kody never paid much attention to trees, but these didn't look like the beech and oak trees she was familiar with. She couldn't even see the road. She rubbed her eyes again, her skin's green glow nearly blinding. Was it getting brighter?

She didn't know what to be more worried about, her apparent arrival in an unknown forest or her deepest secret glowing like a night light and threatening to show the world what a freak she really was.

Pulling her hood down over her hair, she stood on wobbly feet. Every cell in her body felt alive and on edge. She couldn't sit in one place a moment longer. There didn't seem to be a break in the surrounding brush, and looking up, there wasn't even a Kody-shaped hole in the leaves above. What could have happened? Had she passed out? Been kidnapped or abducted by aliens?

The thought made her grin, and she took another deep breath, steadying herself. She could make a plan and figure this out. She pulled her phone out and groaned. There was no signal. She *always* had a signal in the city. She didn't even know how far she'd have to travel to lose a signal. Surely farther than she'd ever been before.

She could try calling out, but then the aliens or kidnappers might have an easier time finding her. She wiped her sleeve across her forehead and grimaced at the smudge of foundation. It was hot. Much hotter than the early spring afternoon she dressed for. Had she lost time as well as distance in passing out?

Maybe she really had fallen into traffic and cracked open her head, and now here she was, months or years later on a hike where she'd fallen and had a memory lapse.

Kody dabbed at the sweat on her forehead again. She couldn't stand here thinking up crazy events. She looked around one more time, picked the direction where the trees looked furthest apart, and started walking.

See? A plan was all she needed.

As she set out, she felt like a looming presence watched her, but no matter how many times she looked over her shoulder, she was alone. The forest was . . . weird. The constant chirp of birds and squirrels dropping acorns or rustling through dry leaves didn't help her paranoia. A branch snapped behind her and she flinched and spun around, but all she could make out through the dense trees was a green deer. At least, she thought it was a green deer. She laid her face in her hands. Aliens seemed more likely by the minute.

Trekking through a forest wasn't easy. Her sneakers weren't up for the damp ground, and her jeans barely protected her legs from branches and brambles. Some plants seemed as sharp as steel, and others felt like they reached out to snare her all on their own. If Kody were superstitious, she might believe the forest was working against her. As it was, she was sticking to her plan. Walk, walk, walk, and walk some more. Eventually the forest had to end, the city girl reasoned.

After a hard twenty-minute walk, Kody stopped and leaned against a tree with chalky white bark to catch her breath. Something stabbed her neck. Careful exploration found a long thorny vine caught in her curls from when she'd ripped away from a bush. Thorns covered her sleeves and pants and her skin underneath felt chewed up and raw. She checked her phone for a signal again and, disappointed, she picked thorns out of her clothes for a few more minutes. The date and time on her phone seemed accurate for when she'd left her apartment and started her walk to the coffee shop, so she couldn't have lost more than a few minutes, definitely not weeks or months, to explain the weather. Weren't forests supposed to be cool with all the shade?

Kody needed to get back to town and figure out what to do about Roger. She needed to call the cops and politely ask someone to escort her to her old apartment so she could collect her things, and then she needed to find a cheap place to sleep for a few days.

She walked for a few hours until the only light shone from her green swirls and she stumbled often in the gloom. Kody knew how to survive on a city street after dark, she knew how to spot someone who was up to no good, and she had a pretty intimidating leer that could scare off an inexperienced mugger. Yet when it came to outdoor skills, she was lost. She didn't know what plants were edible, and she was hungry enough after a long day to start eyeing up a bush like it was a salad bar.

She was undeniably lost and sleeping under a tree, even if it wasn't a particularly nice tree, was better than stumbling into another thorny bush.

In the night, things rustled and stomped through the leaves around her. At one point something large and shadowy sniffled her hair just as she drifted off, but by the time she cast her glow around, the creature was gone, and the forest was still.

She didn't sleep well, and by morning her glow had dimmed, leaving her streaks deeper and more noticeable than they'd been before, as if the glow had brightened their natural hue. Kody fought tears. Passing for normal was hard enough when they'd been faint. She ran a hand over a bright swirl, wincing when her finger grazed one of many deep scratches from her journey the day before.

When the light was bright enough to see by, Kody resumed her walk, stumbling and wincing the first few steps as her sore muscles remembered how to move and her many cuts reopened.

Peeing in the forest wasn't fun. Pee liked to splash, and knowing how to stand was a learning curve she hadn't enjoyed figuring out. Luckily, she'd woken up parched, so dehydration would soon prevent the need for more breezy bathroom breaks.

After an hour she was dragging, her feet catching on every stick and vine, with even more reaching out to cut her flesh and halt her progress. So when the trees thinned and a path formed, she worried she imagined it. But hope spurred her on, and by midmorning the sun was shining brighter through the treetops. She was *almost* positive she was nearing the end. Her eyes strained and played tricks on her as she peered through the trunks, seeking a path. It was as if the trees moved and realigned, filling gaps and hiding any hints that the forest edge was near. When at last she spotted gaps between the trees where more trees didn't immediately appear, her heart leapt and she took off at a jog.

A sneaky vine caught hold of her shoe. Kody went flying and landed on a stinging fern. Her cheek took the brunt of the damage, and she carefully extracted herself from the mess. The wound burned as she carefully traversed the last few feet past the thick trunks and into a meadow rolling into the distance.

Relief and anxiety warred in her chest as she trudged to the closest hill. Turning back to the forest, she let out a deep breath. The trees cut a stark line across the horizon, like an impenetrable barrier to the world. Nowhere could she see a break in the trees for power lines or roads. How she had made it out, she wasn't sure she would ever know.

At the top of the hill, the anxiety in Kody's chest grew, squeezing her heart in a vice-like grip. There were no highways or gas stations, abandoned cars or skyscrapers in the distance. Instead, fluffy white sheep dotted a far hill and a dirt road trailed off to the left. A dilapidated barn sat on another hill, but she thought it was more likely to hold a horde of serial killers than actual farm equipment. Off to the right, far in the distance, there was a mass of structures. She blinked.

It looked almost like a castle at the very center of a large sweeping town, but she couldn't be sure. Kody shook her head at the absurdity of it all and started toward the dirt path, hoping it led toward civilization.

Chapter Three

Kody wasn't a quitter. She was very fond of refusing something she didn't want to do, but if she said yes, she always followed through. It was why her planning was always successful. She didn't stop until it was, or a better plan presented itself. Her current plan—reach civilization, find a phone or computer, book a plane ticket home—was looking less and less likely by the moment.

Physically, she was exhausted, hungry, achy, and dying from the heat, no longer protected from the sun by the forest. Mentally, she was overwhelmed, confused, and disoriented. Emotionally, she was one inconvenience away from a full on break down. Walking to town was the hardest thing Kody had ever done. But eventually she made it.

The town was not a town. It was some weird renaissance reenactment where no one spoke English. Or maybe it was a movie set, but they were filming with unseen drones. It was too high-budget to be a festival, and she couldn't see a pair of New Balance sneakers in sight. Every sword or blade hanging from a belt or horse looked authentic. The buildings and shops around her were dug into the cobblestones, and everything was weather-worn and spoke of age and quality. Kody could easily believe she'd been transported to some remote northern European village, but there were too many people of too many pigments. Only villages in woke-fantasy movies had people of so many shades of brown and creamy pink living together. Still, she didn't see any green people. She pulled her hood further over her head, trying to hide as much of her face as she could, and approached a good-natured looking redhead minding a flower stall.

"Hello, do you speak English?" Kody asked.

The woman said something in a language Kody couldn't identify.

Kody frowned and tried again. "English? I know a little Spanish maybe if that works too. Habla español?"

The woman frowned and shook her head. She spoke again but switched tones halfway through, as if trying a different language as well.

Kody shook her head. "No, sorry. I don't know that one either."

The woman ducked her head as if trying to get a better look at Kody's face, but she turned away before the woman could see any green showing through her day-old foundation. A gray-haired man stood a few paces away, watching their exchange, and Kody nodded to him.

"Hello, do you speak English?"

The man frowned and said something to her before scowling at the flower seller and shouting.

Kody ducked her head and moved a few stalls away before looking back, but the arguing pair were out of sight. She kept walking. When she spotted someone with an open or friendly face, she stopped and asked if they spoke English, trying her hardest to keep the green on her face and hands hidden, but it was hot and her hair stuck to the dripping sweat on her face.

She needed water and would have stuck her head into one of the rain barrels she spotted at building corners if she hadn't seen a sweaty and dusty man do the same.

After trying to converse with another confused-looking worker at a stall, she decided her plan was not working, and she needed to rethink. She paused in the middle of the road, then jumped to the side to make way for a cart as a light airy breeze stirred her hair. She took in a deep breath of relief and turned toward a dark doorway where the faint cool waft of air conditioning beckoned her closer. Before she knew it, her feet crossed the doorway, and she squinted through the darkness of the room. She didn't need her eyes to adjust to the lighting to know what corner the air conditioner was sitting in. She moved around tables and chairs, people eating or drinking and chatting politely in the language she'd had buzzing in her ears all day.

The AC unit or whatever it was, spun vertical fan blades in a mesmerizing pattern as cold air thrust out from the center. The lights of the room flashed off the metal blades, causing a lovely light show. It was as if blue fire slid and moved over the blades like magic. Kody smiled to herself at the absurd thought. She eased back her hood carefully, wishing to take off her hoodie entirely. She wanted to ball up her hair and let the cool hit the back of her neck, but she couldn't. Not in this room full of people, some of which were surely watching her soak in the AC without paying. She took a deep breath of cool air and started counting in her head. How long could she stand there blocking the air before someone yelled at her to move? Not that she would understand if someone did.

She smiled wider and chuckled once, delirious with crisp, cold air.

Someone said something behind her, and she jumped. Kody turned, face-to-face with a brown-eyed, blonde woman, grinning widely while carrying two trays heavy with bowls.

The woman clearly expected Kody to respond. When Kody failed, the woman's grin melted into a slight frown and she said something else.

"Sorry, I don't understand. Do you speak English?"

The woman frowned and stepped forward, looking at something on Kody's face. Kody jumped back and yanked on her hood. She spun around toward the door. A larger man with an apron stood in her path, peering oddly at her, along with a dozen or so diners.

"Uh, hello." Kody gave a little wave, then balled up her fist to cover the green swirl on her palm and shoved it into her pocket. "I'm just gonna go now."

She moved around the man and made it through the door without another glance. The heat smacked her in the face as the glaring sun blazed above. She shielded her eyes and face as she tried to navigate away from the watching eyes.

"Hellooo, helloo," a voice called behind her.

Kody froze, afraid to turn and find the heavily accented English was all another delusion.

A hand wrapped around her arm, and Kody flinched. When she looked up, a man her age with light hair and a tawny complexion looked back. He released her and waved his hands in the air, saying something in the same language as all the others.

Kody shook her head. "I don't understand."

The man held up his hands again, as if asking her to wait. "Hello," he said again, this time slow and careful to pronounce it right.

"Hello," Kody copied and nodded. "Do you speak English?"

The man grinned and lifted his arms before saying something she didn't understand. "Hello, uh"—he stammered for a moment —"Damn. Crap. Uh, toilet!" He yelled a few more colorful curse words, then said a few things in the other language and laughed. "I. Like. Beer!"

He laughed again, this time bending at the waist with mirth.

"You know a little English, then?" Kody asked, smiling carefully.

The man laughed and reached for her arm again. Kody flinched, and he ducked his head and held up his hands. "Helloo," he said, and switched to his language, saying a few things and waving for her to follow him as he turned. "Helloo."

"Okay." Kody held up her hands. "I'll follow you, but I'm not going anywhere creepy."

The man nodded. "Helloo." He grabbed her hand and pulled her down the road.

"Hey! Let go. I'm not interested in getting human trafficked today."

Kody dug in her heels and the man frowned and gave her a few more tugs. "Hello helloo," he said, before tugging her again.

Kody pulled her hand free and gestured for him to continue. He did, but he kept an eye on her as he led her past vendors and down a few well-populated streets. The man stopped and waved her on with a "helloo" if she lagged too far back.

"I'm coming, I'm coming. As long as you don't lead me anywhere that looks too murdery," Kody grumbled under her breath.

After a good five-minute walk through the hot dusty street, the man stepped between two small buildings where a lot of noise was being generated. Kody paused. The sun was bright on the other side of the buildings while the path lay in deep shadow where anything could be lurking. It seemed a little risky. The man stopped again and gestured wildly for her to continue.

"Hello, hello." He continued to speak in whatever language she didn't understand.

Kody stopped and crossed her arms. "Look, I don't know where you're taking me, and we've already gone very far. You could be anybody. You could be somebody trying to kill me or traffic me and I didn't walk all this way just to end up in some murder dungeon."

The man deflated and slumped over. He held up his hand as if asking her to wait and disappeared around the building.

Kody glanced from her right to her left. Was it safer on this side of the dark path? They'd left the main road, and she was all alone behind a row of shops, where she couldn't hear any foot traffic over the noise coming from whatever lay beyond the dark path. He could just as easily be fetching a large group of people to come up and attack her.

The hair on the back of her neck rose, but she decided to risk it. She stepped into the gloom between the two buildings and waited for her eyes to adjust. Squinting, it looked like the path opened into a clear courtyard and the sounds that before had just seemed like noise broke themselves up into more industrial sounds. Banging, hammering, sawing. Just a few more steps and her location became obvious as men and women wandered about completing laborious tasks. There was a man stretching long hides over two sticks, a woman running a metal box over the top of a wood board producing long strips of wood chips, and all other sorts of workers. No one did more than glance up from their work or nod to her casually before returning to their tasks.

A familiar voice grew loud to her left in that unknown language, and Kody turned toward several blacksmith forges. One of which had her guide standing in the entrance, gesturing wildly between her and the man he spoke to.

The new man wielded a large hammer and pounded a strip of metal as if oblivious to the man yelling at him. The forge was dimly lit compared to the courtyard and Kody could barely make out the new man's form except to see he had an expanse of sweaty, light skin and was definitely not wearing a shirt.

Kody's guide raised his voice again and tried to grab the hammer from the blacksmith, but it was too heavy and unbalanced them both. The blacksmith yelled as several small metal things crashed into the ground and a bucket of water toppled over and rushed out of the stall. A female blacksmith working in the next stall over yelled something that sounded like a nasty curse, and a young boy helping her used a broom to guide the water out of her stall and into a gutter lining the courtyard.

The blacksmith spat what were obviously curses to Kody's guide and bent over, picking up the metal bits that dropped. Kody's guide yelled back and slapped the fallen pieces from the blacksmith's hands. Kody flinched, expecting the blacksmith to get angry. He was taller and more powerfully built than her guide, and it would take much less energy than lifting that hammer to knock her guide to the ground.

But the blacksmith didn't raise his hands or try to hit Kody's guide. Instead, he seemed to deflate a little and just looked him, lifting his hands as if to say 'what.' The guide gestured again toward Kody.

The blacksmith barely glanced at her before shaking his head and muttering something. The guide nodded enthusiastically and grabbed the blacksmith's arm, pulling him into the courtyard.

As the blacksmith stepped into the light of the courtyard, Kody had to take a breath. He was tall and lean, but his arms and chest were sculpted with powerful muscles, clearly on display for all to see, as if in no doubt they were a gift to the world. His skin was light with an olive tone, and his hair was a mop of long chestnut locks hanging in his eyes. This man was handsome in a way Kody had often seen on TV and movies but rarely in person. His dark eyes had an edge to them that spoke of a troubled past. Perfect for luring in soft-hearted women who just wanted a man they could fix. But his gorgeous exterior didn't fool her. She knew a man who looked like that on the outside definitely had a gooey jerk filling, and life had too many problems to add more just for the sake of a pretty face or body. She crossed her arms, unwilling to be swayed by the impressive blacksmith.

The blacksmith, on the other hand, didn't seem to notice her indecision over his looks. Instead, he argued with Kody's guide, barely sparing her a glance.

Right. It's not like anyone who looked like him would be interested in her.

The guide turned to her and started gesturing again. "Hello, helloo," he said, as if expecting her to jump into their conversation.

Kody rolled her eyes. "I don't understand what you're saying."

At her words, the blacksmith's eyebrows shot up and he glanced at her with his pretty caramel eyes. Ugh. Life just wasn't fair.

"You speak English?" The blacksmith asked, and Kody nearly exploded with hope as she bent with relief.

Chapter Four

"Yes! Yes I do! Please help, I have absolutely no idea where I am or how I got here" —No need to mention the weird lights or the spinning as she fell into the road and landed in a forest— "I just need to get back home. I live in Pittsburgh and can book a flight or something, if you have a phone I can borrow."

The blacksmith stared at her blankly. Had she spoken too fast? Maybe his English wasn't that good, though he didn't sound like he had an accent.

"I need to go home," she said again slowly. "Pittsburgh, in the United States."

The blacksmith shook his head. "You can't get there from here. Have you met Thomas? He orbed me last fall and said he found all of you."

Kody blinked. She understood most of the words he'd used, but the meaning escaped her. "I don't think I know Thomas." Maybe she'd gone to school with one or two but didn't think that counted.

"Of course not." The blacksmith rolled his eyes and flipped his bangs out of his face. The gesture had too cool for school written all over it. He sighed and looked around. "I have an orb in my room. Let me go grab it and he can explain this to you." He said something to her guide, who ducked into the stall.

"Explain what? What are you talking about? Wait, don't leave me."

The blacksmith turned toward a door in the side of the building behind the forge, and Kody hurried to follow before the one person who spoke English could disappear.

He glanced back at her and sighed.

Out of the sun was cooler, but Kody was disappointed the building didn't have an AC. The door led to a short hall with a few closed doors and a staircase, which the blacksmith climbed. It was dim after the bright sun, but weird light bulbs hung on the walls every few steps, lighting the way.

They reached the second floor, then ascended to the third. Kody was panting by the time she touched the last step and forced her legs to follow the blacksmith down the hall. She needed food. She needed water. She needed a bed. She wasn't built for any of this. The blacksmith stopped in front of one of the many doors lining the hall, and it was all Kody could do not to collapse against the wall while she waited for the man to pull out a key, which he didn't do.

He grabbed the doorknob and held it for a moment longer than normal before turning the knob. He opened the door and gestured for Kody to enter. Thick, dark curtains covered the windows, blocking out the heat and light, but the room was nearly cool. A bookshelf lined one wall next to a small desk, and a table with two chairs sat in the far corner. She spotted a couch on one wall and collapsed onto it while the blacksmith moved around the room and turned on lamps with a touch. Or not lamps, but more of those odd light bulbs that didn't seem to have any wires as they stuck out from the wall. He paused near a desk and pulled a shirt off a chair. Kody tried not to look disappointed as he put it on before digging through the desk's drawers.

"The tea is cold, but there's water on the table if you want it," the blacksmith said, gesturing to a small side table next to an open door.

Kody ran for it.

A large pitcher, blue with little white flowers painted on the side, sat next to a teapot, a dirty teacup, and an empty wood cup. She didn't care if it was clean. She filled the cup and drained it in a long drag that would make any frat guy envious. Halfway through a third cup, her stomach felt ready to burst and she noticed the blacksmith watching her, eyes raised and mouth hanging open.

Kody ducked her head and wiped her face before glancing back at the gorgeous guy. His expression had changed to sheepish as he played with something in his hands.

"Sorry, I guess I could be a better host. I'm just not very good at this stuff. How long ago did you arrive?" he asked.

"Yesterday. I woke up in a forest or something." Kody's eyes strayed to the open door next to her, through which she spotted a bed, messy and rumpled with clothes strewn about. She diverted her gaze back to the blacksmith.

"A forest?" He laughed once. "No, more likely it was a thick batch of trees. There aren't any true forests a day's walk from here where you would have landed."

Annoyance flashed in Kody, and she swallowed her first reply. "Trust me, it was a forest. It took me over a day to get out of it."

The man frowned. "The only batch of woods that big is to the east, and that's impossible."

"Whatever you say," Kody agreed. She wasn't about to argue about where she'd been with this man when she didn't even know what country she was in.

The man straightened and looked awkward for a moment. "Uh, shall we sit while I make a call?"

Kody sighed. "Yes please. Or just give me your phone and I can make a call myself." Though who she'd call, she wasn't sure. She fell onto the couch and the man sat on the edge at the farthest point from her.

"It's not that kind of call," he said and held up a glass ball. He wrapped his long fingers around it and held it close for a moment, and the ball flashed colors before he relaxed his grip and let it rest in his palm. A picture appeared in the center of the glass.

Oh great. A magician with a crystal ball. Just what Kody needed.

"Hey, Tristan. What's up, my man?"

Kody startled at the voice and leaned forward for a better look at the glass. A face peered out of the ball, brown eyes, dark brown skin and a curly cap of hair, the entire picture warped slightly by the sphere.

"Hey Thomas, I thought you said you found all the Misplaced?" Tristan said.

Tristan. What a weirdly normal name for Kody's delusion to possess. She must be laying in a hospital somewhere, her skull cracked open, and a nice medical team trying to scoop her brains back inside as she hallucinated vividly about a gorgeous blacksmith with a frickin crystal ball.

"Yeah, because I did," Thomas, the man trapped in the magical crystal ball, replied.

"Well, I think you missed one," Tristan said. "I have a girl here that a friend found wandering through the market. She said she's been walking since yesterday, which might get her to the border of Aluna."

The orb guy was quiet for a long moment. "Maybe Elodie has an illegitimate sister she doesn't know about."

"Yeah, or the king of Rohap didn't know he had an heir." Tristan scratched his neck and glanced awkwardly at Kody.

"What's her name?" Thomas asked.

"Uh, what's your name?" he asked her.

"She's there? Why didn't you introduce her? And why haven't you asked her her name yet?"

Tristan sighed and held out his hand and the glass ball. "Here, you talk to him."

"What?" Kody asked, pulling her hands away.

"This is Thomas. He's good at explaining things. Take the orb and talk to him. It's just like FaceTime, except it's round and powered by magic."

"Magic?" Kody squeaked.

Tristan grabbed her sleeve and dropped the ball into her hand. It was smooth and heavy in her palm.

Kody ducked her shoulders and held the ball up. "Hello?" she said into it.

"Hi. You can just talk normal," Thomas said. "Sorry I didn't see you before. Tristan is a little short on manners. My name is Thomas. I grew up in Illinois, though I wasn't born there. My sister Kat and I were in foster care there. She was adopted young, but I grew up in the system. Are you a foster or adopted kid?"

It wasn't a yes or no question. He was asking her which one, as if he knew she was one or the other.

"I was in foster care. In Pittsburgh."

Tristan rose from his seat and crossed the room to the water pitcher. He refilled the cup Kody used.

"Pennsylvania, nice. I've visited Philadelphia a few times," Thomas said.

"How did you know?" Kody asked softly.

"Because we all were. All twenty-six of us. Well, twenty-seven with you. We're known as the Misplaced. It means we are misplaced from time or the world. There were twenty-seven of us, all babies, who were pulled out of our lives by the whims of a madman and dropped on Earth, where we were shuffled into various public services."

Tristan returned with the water and handed it to her. She took a few big gulps, surprised her stomach could hold it. She set it on a small table next to the couch.

"You know this sounds crazy, don't you?"

Thomas laughed. "Yeah, I do. Some of us have stories like that, people thinking we were crazy for believing we weren't from that world and labeling us as troublemakers. Some of us, like Tristan and I, traveled back and forth from Earth to this world, Eres, while growing up. Others, like you, never traveled until the spell was broken. If you get up the courage, you can ask Tristan his story."

Tristan rolled his eyes and fell back against the couch.

"But you have to agree this world doesn't feel like the one you're used to, does it?" Thomas asked.

Kody didn't have to think to know that answer. It didn't. From the air that felt alive, flowing around her since the moment she'd landed, making her swirls glow, to the people and village so uniquely alien and unlike anything in her modern world.

"It's not possible," she said, shaking her head.

"No, and neither is talking to someone through a glass ball. Look, I know this is all weird, but before you know it, this place will feel like home. We'll find where you came from, who your people are, and where you belong. All of us were born a long time ago in this world, so our parents are all long dead, but most of us have someone along the family lines still waiting for us."

Kody shook her head. She'd grown out of dreaming about her birth family, all foster kids did eventually. She didn't need this starry-eyed man giving her false hope. "So how do I get back? I already missed work, and I have things I need to deal with." She needed to call the cops before the proof of her occupancy in her apartment went up in flames.

"You can't go back. I'm sorry if that's shocking, but this is where you live now. We were trapped on Earth, but the spell was broken and we are all here now. The spell broke two years ago and everyone like you who remained trapped has now traveled back here over that time. You're the last. This is your home. It's where you were born and where you belong."

Kody's head spun. It wasn't like she had a lot to get back to, but what she had she'd fought for. If she didn't go back, it would be like Roger won.

But maybe this meant Roger didn't even matter anymore.

She shook her head and ran a hand over her face. “Why should I believe any of this?”

She glanced at Tristan, who was frowning at her.

“You don’t have to,” Thomas said. “You can just keep on living, thinking this is all made up and waiting for the truth to shine through. It won’t and eventually you’ll see that. But if it’s easier to live with, go for it.”

Tristan reached over to her, and Kody held up the orb, thinking he would take it. Instead, he snatched her hand. She tried to pull it back, but his grip was firm.

“So what’s next? Tristan, do I need to make arrangements for our new friend? I’m sure Graham can spare a room.”

Tristan pulled Kody’s hand closer and glanced up, a shocked look on his face. He plucked a light bulb off the wall. Kody blinked. It wasn’t exactly a light bulb, more like another glass sphere filled with light. It mesmerized her long enough that she didn’t protest as Tristan moved the light over her hand and tugged up her sleeve, clearly revealing the green spiral traveling up her arm.

“You said you landed in the forest?” Tristan asked.

“What about a forest?” Thomas asked.

Kody nodded. Heat shot up her arm and into her cheeks, still partially shielded from view, with her hair and hood firmly obscuring her face. She wasn’t sure if it was fear at his discovery or something else that made her pulse beat.

“What’s going on?” Thomas asked.

“Nothing,” Tristan said. He released her hand and snatched the ball from Kody. “Thanks for the explanation, Thomas. I can take it from here.” He squeezed the ball again, and Thomas’s confused face winked out.

Tristan dropped the ball on the couch and leaned closer to Kody. She froze, not sure what to do. Would he think she was weird? Or maybe being partially green in his world was bad and he would hate her.

But as he leaned closer, his long fingers reached for her hood and pushed it back; hate was the last thing on his face. Carefully, he pushed at the mess of hair, her unruly curls now tied in frizzy knots, until he could see more of her face. Her cheeks burned and her entire world seemed to hinge on what he would say next.

"You're Elvman."

Well, that wasn't what she was expecting.

"I'm sorry?"

He pushed her hair back further and ran a finger over her ear and its awkward arch that she usually tried to cover with her hair. He smiled. "Well, maybe not full Elv. But you're definitely one of them." He sat back, and Kody could breathe again. "That's why you landed in the forest. The forest isn't part of the Twoshy, it's its own land all to itself, and rumors say it holds an Elv kingdom, the last Kingdom of the Elv. You must be their princess."

Chapter Five

The warm, tingly feelings that had slithered their way over Kody's body at his touch abruptly ended.

"I'm sorry. Did you just say I'm an elf princess?"

Tristan chuckled, and it was really enjoyable to watch. "No, Elv, short for Elvman. In this world, there are four races of men. Human, Elvman, Dwarvman, and Aviman. Human are basically the same as on Earth, except here, on Eres, some can do magic. Human mages made that orb and these light globes." He gestured first to the crystal ball that held Thomas's face and then tossed the glowing light ball in the air before sticking it back to the wall. "Mages created all the technological advances we have here, like working plumbing. We even have showers." He gestured to a closed door in the same wall as the bedroom.

He stood and made his way to the closed door.

"Where are you going?" she asked stupidly. He had just told her it was the bathroom.

"Just a moment," he said.

Kody tried to look busy. She pulled out her phone and booted it up to check for a signal just to make sure these men weren't lying to her.

Tristan didn't close the door, and Kody tried not to listen, although all she heard was the sound of running water and the opening and closing of a cabinet. He returned a short time later with a bowl of warm water and a bag. He moved the side table over and set his things on it within easy reach.

"Take off your jacket," he said as he sat next to her again.

"What?" Kody wasn't sure what she was expecting, but it wasn't that.

"It's full of holes and your face is scratched up. I want to patch everything up before you get an infection." He readied things on the table, pulling out strips of clean white cloth and small bottles and jars. Kody focused on his hands while he worked. His hands and arms had been streaked with sweat and soot from his work in the forge, but now even his fingernails were clean, as if he worked an office job or something. When she didn't move, he glanced at her. "Well?"

Her brain had a hard time coming up with a witty comeback, so she settled on a partial truth. "I stink."

He rolled his eyes. "I work in a hot forge. Sweat and BO don't bother me. Some plants here are poisonous and others are magical. I'd rather take care of things now before I have to carry you to a mage for healing."

Was there any way for her to avoid it? He hadn't seemed repulsed at the green on her hand and face, but she still didn't want to bare her arms to the light of day. She didn't even want to see how bright the pattern had gotten.

She sighed and pulled off her hoodie. The relief of the cooler air reaching her body was immediate, but she averted her eyes from her own arms while she pulled back her hair. "Do you have something I can tie my hair up in?"

Tristan left and returned with a length of leather cord, and folded striped fabric. She unfolded it to find a pair of boxers. She glanced at Tristan, who was scratching the back of his neck and not looking at her.

"I don't have any shorts, but your jeans are ripped to shreds."

"Right." Kody rose and escaped into the bathroom. It was surprisingly clean. Cleaner than she kept hers, which was always a challenge, with Roger being an absolute slob. When they first moved in together, she cleaned every day, wiping beard shavings off the bathroom sink, cleaning pee splatter from the toilet, making sure every dish in the house was washed after every meal. But somewhere in the last few months, she'd given up and let the house fall into a low level state of grime. But this bathroom . . . Someone else had to clean this for Tristan. No way was he so clean. The white porcelain and the blue pastel tile shone. The large mirror bore a simple design with a set of drawers under the sink and a shelf filled with fluffy white towels over the toilet. One side of the bathroom was dedicated to the toilet, while the other housed a deep bathtub and—pulling back the slate curtain—a shower.

Kody suddenly felt filthy.

She poked her head out of the bathroom.

"Do you care if I take a shower instead?"

"No, go for it," Tristan replied. Kody grinned and closed the door, but a moment later Tristan's voice came through the door, closer than he'd been before. "Actually, take a long one and I will see if I can get some spare clothes for you."

Kody opened the door to reply just as the apartment door closed behind Tristan. She shrugged and closed the door. Peeling off her clothes, still damp with sweat, she dropped them on the floor. No, that made her feel like a slob. She folded each piece, tucking her under things between her jeans and shirt. Turning to the shower, Kody glimpsed herself in the mirror and froze.

She tried not to look at her unclothed body too often, maybe a monthly or bimonthly glance to make sure nothing weird was growing, but things had changed drastically since her last inspection. Faint green no longer applied. Her swirls were deep, vibrant green, like fresh pine needles swirling around the rich brown of her normal pinecone colored skin. Cuts and scratches ruined the elegance, but she could make out the design and flow of her lines like never before, and for a moment, it was beautiful.

She closed her eyes and turned from the mirror. It wasn't beautiful, it was weird and abnormal. She turned on the water and waited for it to get warm before stepping into the deep tub. Pulling the thick curtain closed cloaked her in darkness, and she thought that would do well to avoid another sight of the horrid green.

Why had her skin transformed with her arrival to this world? Maybe someone here would know how to make it go back the way it was or remove the green all together. If Elvman were real, maybe one of them would know.

The warm water had perfect pressure, but it wasn't quite refreshing. Kody turned down the temperature and basked in the cool shower after her sweaty day in the sun. The stream of water felt wonderful against her shoulders but stung something fierce when it encountered one of the many cuts along her arms and legs.

A large glass bottle and a bar of soap were the only products in the shower. The soap smelled like peppermint and made her think of Tristan. He was hard to get a read on, distant and cold one moment and intense and focused the next. He was rude, like he wished he didn't have to deal with her, but then brought her water, and offered to find her clothes.

She didn't feel exactly safe in this new world, but she didn't think he was the sort to resort to violence, despite his obvious strength.

Kody ducked her face under the water and attempted to wash the thoughts from her head. She didn't need a rebound or to become obsessed with a guy who probably had a handful of girls at his beck and call.

She spent a long time working sticks and twigs out of her curls with the bar of soap and a comb she found in the drawer under the sink while snooping before Tristan returned and knocked on the bathroom door. She stuck her head out of the curtain. "Yeah?"

Tristan opened the door a crack and shoved clothes and a sack through the gap, setting everything carefully on the tile. His eyes were closed and Kody couldn't help but smile. "Uh, I got some clothes and some, um, hair products and other things. I'm just gonna set them right in here. She gave me like, three kinds of conditioners or something. The red one is a wash-out, and the blue is leave-in. And there's a cream. I don't know what it's for, but my neighbor said it was important."

Kody covered her smile, trying not to laugh. "Thanks, I think I can figure it out."

"Okay, I'll be . . . not in here."

"Sounds good."

When the door closed, Kody stepped out of the tub and dripped on the mat while digging through the bag. There were several bottles and a jar, along with a toothbrush, and what she suspected was a bundle of feminine hygiene products.

She couldn't help her "awww" when she realized he'd gotten her pads, just in case. He couldn't be that perfect, could he?

She finished her shower, infinitely faster and easier with the proper hair products, and wrapped a towel around her body and a second around her hair. Then she set to work cleaning the shower of hair and leaves and wiping up the water she'd gotten everywhere. She cleaned and dried his comb and stuck it back in the drawer, then inspected the other contents of his cabinet. She found something in a jar that reminded her of an all-natural deodorant one of her old roommates had made, and she smeared it on her armpits before using something she was nearly positive was a dissolvable toothpaste tablet to brush her teeth. Another bottle proved to be lotion, and Kody coated her skin, half mesmerized and half disgusted by how her freshly moisturized green skin glowed in the magical lights.

At last she dug through the clothes and found something resembling a sports bra and a pair of orange underwear. For pants, there were lightweight brown trousers, made of something like linen or cotton, that were loose over her legs. They felt intentionally loose but synched at the waist with a long drawstring that hung halfway down her thigh. The shirt was flowy and yellow with short sleeves. It would be perfect for the weather, but Kody didn't think she could handle so much skin showing, even if yellow did compliment her green nicely. It was all more color than she ever wore, and though everything was lovely, she cringed at not being able to blend into the background.

Wanting to stall emerging from the bathroom for as long as possible, she took the towel off her hair and fussed with her curls until they came back to life, and she again felt like herself.

She glanced in the mirror to make sure everything was in place and didn't recognize herself. Her hair looked the same, but everything else was different. Every day for ten years she smothered herself in foundation, and now without it a stranger looked back at her. Her swirls came up each side of her face and flowed over her cheeks and across her nose. Another swirl arched over one eyebrow and across her forehead as others wound over her chin and around her neck. Scratches covered her face and neck, breaking the flow of green. She took a deep breath and met her eyes. They had always been that odd green-brown mix of hazel, but now the green overwhelmed the brown, and in spots the green nearly shimmered, but maybe that was the light.

She could never go back, her life was over. Even if Tristan didn't say it was impossible, there was no way to hide how different she'd become. Long sleeves and foundation wouldn't be enough. She'd need gloves and the sort of thick concealer people used to hide tattoos.

Kody pulled her eyes away from the mirror. She'd seen enough.

Chapter Six

Finished in the bathroom, Kody took a deep breath. Tristan would provide the information she needed about how this world worked and what she could expect, and she would make a plan on what to do next. Centered and focused again, she stepped back out into the sitting room. Tristan wasn't there.

A thump came from the bedroom, and Kody glanced through the door. Tristan stretched out a sheet on the bed and jumped when he noticed her.

"Sorry, I wasn't sure what to do with my dirty things," Kody said, holding up the bundle of her clothes.

"Right, you can toss them in the hamper over there." He gestured to a basket with soot-streaked clothes piled high, sitting between a wardrobe and coat rack. "The building has a laundry service." Tristan threw a blanket into the air over the bed and smoothed it into place. Kody unfurled a corner and helped him stuff pillows into clean cases. It embarrassed her at how much her heart raced while making a bed, the only bed in the apartment, with a handsome and kind stranger. She fought hard to keep her mind surface level and not let it run away to places better not thought of in mixed company.

She tossed the pillow at the head of the bed and glanced at Tristan. He watched her as he covered the last pillow, but looked away when she noticed.

"If you're okay with it, you can sleep in here and I can take the couch." He grabbed a second blanket and a pillow and headed for the bedroom door. The little flame that danced merrily in the middle of Kody's chest went out. He looked back at her. "If you aren't comfortable here, I have a friend who runs an inn in town. He's a good man, but that place is usually packed."

"I would prefer here, if that's okay," Kody said quickly. "I don't want to take your bed, though. I can sleep on the couch."

She tried to take the blanket from him, but he snorted and moved around her to the living room.

"Please, I keep early hours at the forge. You'll be more comfortable in the room." He gestured to the couch. "Have a seat so I can look at your cuts."

"They're fine. I washed everything out well."

"I can see two from here that look inflamed. Sit."

Kody sat.

Tristan disappeared into the bathroom again to wash his hands before joining her on the couch and sitting a little too close. He opened a jar and the chaotic scent of an essential oils shop hit her.

"Wow, that's strong."

The edge of Tristan's mouth curved into a brief grin. "Sometimes magic used to enhance the strength of something enhances more than just the healing effects. But don't worry. You should only smell like a spice cabinet for a few hours."

Tristan dipped his finger in the cream and held out his hand.

Kody placed her hand in his, and he pulled her arm closer.

"So this is some magical ointment, then?" She winced when he dabbed the cream on the largest cut on her forearm. It stung for a long moment, then went numb.

"Of course." Tristan looked up at her and grinned. "I know it takes some getting used to, but there are some things about this world that are better than the one you left."

Kody nodded and winced as Tristan moved on to another cut. "That conditioner was fantastic. Who'd you get them from, a girlfriend?"

Tristan hovered over a fresh cut for a moment too long before moving on. "Uh, no, she's taken, and her girlfriend would probably kick my ass if I tried anything."

Kody tried not to grin.

"She said she'd bring by a few more things later today, since one change of clothes won't last you long."

"That's really kind, but I don't have any money."

Tristan gave a small wave of his hand before scooping up more ointment and starting on her other arm. "It's been handled."

"Thanks, but I don't like to owe anyone. Should I be repaying this friend or you?"

Tristan sighed, then pulled up the flowy sleeve of her shirt and plopped ointment on a thick cut that made Kody wince.

"I've spent a lot of my life popping between Earth and this world. On Earth, I was a foster kid, relying on the system for everything. Then I travel here and again I can do nothing but accept charity. There used to be a law that any who encountered one of the Misplaced in need offered what aid they could. That means I've spent most of my life depending on others for everything." He raised his eyebrows. "So believe me when I say I get where you're coming from. I'm not from this city, but I came here and apprenticed with a blacksmith so I could have a trade, so I would never have to accept handouts again. If I now finally have the chance to help someone else, would you take that from me?"

She met his caramel brown eyes and tried her hardest not to melt. Tristan leaned in and brushed her hair behind her ear, which didn't work very well, and lightly ran his finger over a cut on her cheekbone. Kody held her breath while he moved on to her neck and pulled her hair back so he had better access. His fingers flashed over the scratches on her neck and collarbone.

He cleared his throat and grabbed a strip of white cloth. "Let's see if it's working." He dipped the cloth in the bowl of water and rung it out, then lifted the first arm he'd applied ointment to. He turned it, revealing her worst scratch, and Kody blanched.

"What is that?" Something yellow brown and gooey lined the top of her cut, and Tristan wiped it up with a corner of the cloth before folding it and wiping again. The cut under the gunk looked a week old, as if the ointment had hurried her healing. She lifted her arm closer to examine the healing cut. Was it really magic?

"That cut was infected, probably with some plant toxin. The ointment helped your body purge itself." Tristan took her arm back and whipped at another gooey spot.

"Ew, so that's poison you're wiping up?"

"Poison and puss, probably."

"Gross." Kody went to cover her face with a hand, but stopped when she noticed a cut on that hand also gooping. She grimaced. All romantic feelings gone.

Tristan chuckled. "It's normal. I get scratches all the time from metal and things. The cuts that aren't infected will be totally gone by morning, and the others, the morning after that."

"I can't believe I'm in some magical world and supposedly some elf or Elv or whatever."

Tristan chuckled again, and it made her feel a tiny bit better. "What did you think you were before knowing about all of this? I mean, your ears aren't as sharp as a full-blooded Elv, but the green must have been an issue."

She'd never talked about it so openly with anyone before, but what did she have to lose? Tristan could clearly see her, had put his fingers all over her green and brown arms in the bright glow of the magic lights. She took a deep breath. "It wasn't this green before."

Tristan paused and looked up at her again, his eyes so focused as if he could see straight through her. "What do you mean?"

“It started when I was ten. The swirls were only really visible in sunlight, then got a little darker over the years. I used foundation on my face and neck, and wore long sleeves year around, and that pretty much took care of things. It was an oddity, but only something people really close to me ever noticed, and I didn’t let many people that close.”

Tristan nodded and broke his intense eye contact, then returned to wiping her arms clean. “When did it change, then?”

Kody sighed. “When I fell into that stupid forest. My skin started glowing, like the spirals were literally glowing green for hours. When I woke up, the glowing was gone, but they were still this vivid. I don’t think foundation would even cover them now.”

“Well, it’s a good thing you don’t have to cover them anymore.”

“Are you kidding me? I look like a weird candy cane. Why wouldn’t I cover it? I was just thinking how I hope your friend brings me something with long sleeves or I need to get my hoodie washed before I leave this room.”

“Roll up your pant legs for me,” Tristan said, scooting back for a better angle. She did what he said, hoping her cheeks weren’t noticeably blushing. She hadn’t shaved in a while and her legs were badly scratched and welted all the way up her thighs. Tristan didn’t seem to care. He scooped out more ointment before setting to work. “It’s too hot this summer to wear long sleeves for anything other than sun protection. An Elv in town would be an oddity, but other than a few looks, no one is going to bother you. Besides, some people like candy canes.” Tristan looked up at her with a charming smirk, his hand holding her calf. She had to look away as her stomach did little cartwheels.

“How do you know I’m an Elv if no one has ever seen one?”

“It’s not that we never see them, just that it’s rare. They have a long bloody history with the Hu. But people know what they look like. We have a way of telling stories here in the Twoshy. It’s kind of like magical telepathic TV, and people use it to share stories. I’m not good at it, but I’ll take you to one sometime.”

Kody sighed and watched the poison ooze out of her leg cuts with sick satisfaction while she thought. "There's a lot I don't know about this world."

"Well, I can't share a tale, but I can give you a brief history if that helps."

"Anything would help at this point."

Tristan sat up and moved to the floor so he had a better angle to tend to her other leg. "Let me think where to start. I guess the beginning is best. The continent we live on is known as the Kingdom of Sixteen, more commonly called the Twoshy. Back when it was founded, it was mostly occupied by Elvman, Dwarvman, Aviman, and dragons."

"Dragons?"

"Yes," Tristan said with a bemused grin.

"Sorry, go on."

He cleared his throat. "Humankind occupied most of the remaining world. The other races don't like us, so wherever we went they left, until the only place remaining was here."

"Why don't they like us?"

"Knowing what you do of mankind, do you like us?"

Kody said nothing, and Tristan picked up another clean cloth and dampened it.

"So anyway, when this land was all that was left, a bunch of rich selfish Hu got together and invaded. Excuse me, I mean colonized."

Kody chuckled.

"There were sixteen colonies planned, sixteen being seen as a magically strong number, and when they arrived and the war began, there were significant losses on all sides. Two of the leaders died along with a good portion of their people, and so two of the colonies were never established. We ended with fourteen nations, two short of sixteen, hence, we call it the Twoshy."

"Aw, that's catchy."

Tristan grinned. “So the Elv, Avi, Dwarv, and dragons all supposedly left the Twoshy, and the Hu took over.”

“Why supposedly?” Kody asked with a wince as Tristan wiped a particularly nasty gash on her shin. He applied a second coat of ointment to it.

“The Avi took to the mountains and the Elv disappeared, though we hear rumors of them living in the forests, and every now and then there are sightings. The Dwarv are most like the Hu, so some of them integrated, and well, loads of people don’t even realize they have Dwarv blood.”

“What of the dragons?” Kody whispered.

Tristan smiled, and Kody hoped he didn’t notice her heart skip a beat. “People say they left and went to more desolate lands, but I have it on good authority they just moved south, to the other side of the mountains, where most Hu don’t bother to travel.”

“You’re gonna tell me the story you have there, right?”

“Maybe eventually. But we’re getting off track. Back when we were babies, there was a powerful wizard who got pissed off at all our parents, the leaders and rulers of the Twoshy. That’s the other thing us Misplaced have in common. All of our parents were leaders.”

“So you’re a prince?”

“No, my parents were elected officials.” Tristan frowned.

“Oh.”

Something caught Kody’s eye and she frowned. “Your desk drawer is glowing.”

Tristan didn’t even glance over his shoulder. “Probably one of the others trying to get in touch.”

“You mean one of the other Misplaced? Shouldn’t you answer it?”

Tristan shrugged and rubbed more ointment into her leg. “They’re always calling and checking in for no reason. Thomas is probably just fussing.”

“Sounds like they care about you.”

Tristan rolled his shoulders as if uncomfortable with the thought. “They shouldn’t. Just because we were all trapped by the same spell doesn’t mean we’re friends or family.”

Kody understood what he meant. Just because she’d been in the system with other kids didn’t mean they owed each other anything, but she still felt like there was more behind Tristan’s words than a pragmatic worldview. He guarded himself by keeping others at arm’s length, just as Kody wanted to do after her break from Roger.

Kody still wanted to believe intrinsic relationships were possible, she just wasn’t sure she could ever find one.

Eventually, the drawer stopped its pulsating glow.

Tristan continued his history lesson as if nothing had happened. “So this bad wizard casts a spell on all the heirs of the Twoshy and traps them in what we know of as Earth. The heirs being just the babies of the current leaders. It would take too much power to trap older kids or adults, and babies have more of a shock factor.”

“But that doesn’t explain me if the Elv aren’t a part of the Twoshy.”

“I’m getting there. Thomas, the guy from the orb, made it his thing to track us all down, find everyone and help them transition, especially those of us like you who didn’t know what you were until the spell was broken. We thought we had everyone because we were just thinking of those lost from the fourteen nations. And it’s easy enough to tell who is who. We all travel back within the borders of our own lands. I’m from Pundica, which is further west of here. This nation, Rohap, the ruler didn’t have any heirs, so I knew you didn’t belong to this kingdom, and the only other nation within walking distance is to the south, and I know who the Misplaced from there. She’s already happily sitting on a throne and ruling with her new husband.” When he said this, his face grew broody again, and Kody wondered what history existed between him and that queen. Not that Tristan's past mattered to her at all. She was just curious.

"But I came from the forest," Kody reminded him.

"Exactly. The forest that is rumored to be the last city of the Elv. When the wizard cast his spell, he used a map to set the boundary of his magical working. The forest fell within that map, so it makes sense that you were the heir of the forest at the time of the casting, and none of the Hu ever knew about it."

"So, what does that actually mean?"

Tristan finished wiping the last of the cuts on her legs and rested his arm on her knee while he looked up at her. "Elv have long lives. It means that out of all of us Misplaced, all of us orphans, you might be the only one to still have living parents. Family that were alive when you were taken and are still waiting for you."

Chapter Seven

After dropping the bombshell of a potential living family, Tristan cleaned up his supplies and left the small apartment to get them food. He told her the front of the building was a tavern and meals were part of his rent.

Kody didn't know what to think of Tristan's pronouncement. Finding her birth family, hoping for living parents, discovering her birth name, those were all things she'd desperately wanted as a little girl, but as she grew, she knew it was a lost cause, a fantasy. There were so few scenarios that would explain her being in the system and her parents' blameless, loving people who wanted her back. She'd given up as most did, eventually.

Over the last few years, she'd started having a different sort of dream, one where she had a family all her own. Get married, have kids. It was a faraway fuzzy dream, not one she was ready for, and not one she could picture while living with Roger, but it was still a possibility. A chance to create something she'd never had.

She feared that if she reached for that little girl's dream of loving parents who would do anything to have her back, she would be wrecked if it wasn't true, so she put the thought out of her mind. Maybe finding people like her, where for once she truly blended in and didn't have to hide, would be nice, but she wouldn't do it with any hope of finding a family. That she could endure.

Kody spent a few moments looking over her legs, and the nearly healed wounds that had been burning and stinging only a half hour before. Satisfied her legs wouldn't fall off any time soon, she rolled down her pant legs, stood from the couch, and crossed to the desk. She wasn't snooping exactly, but she was bored; it wasn't like Tristan had a TV. The desk was neat and organized, a small stack of papers on one side, a book with a bookmark, in a language she didn't understand. Even the drawers were organized with quills, ink, pencils, paper, and random gadgets like the orb.

She carefully flipped through the loose papers and saw diagrams and schematics for projects she couldn't quite understand. Wheel sketches and mechanical levers covered several pages before something interesting caught her eye. She'd never taken an engineering class, but she knew what a basic engine looked like, though she didn't get how it all fit in a magical world. Some pages had English on them, but nothing that let her make sense of things.

The bookcase was just as unreadable. Novels all in languages she didn't understand, crammed in with more technical engineering books that at least had pictures, but were nonetheless boring.

When Tristan returned with a covered tray, Kody had finished snooping and returned to the couch, trying her phone again for a signal. "Trust me, it won't work," he said by way of greeting.

"It's hard not to keep checking," Kody said with a laugh. "I'm used to having this thing in my hand all day." The smell of bread and roasted meat hit her a moment later, and she closed her mouth so as not to drool all over her new shirt.

"You get used to it, eventually."

Tristan placed the platter on the small table and Kody followed him, eager to dig in. When he lifted the cover, she nearly passed out. A loaf of fluffy bread caught her eye first, followed by some kind of roasted meat, seasoned veggies, and two mugs of soup. Kody snatched up a mug and took a careful temperature check before gulping down the creamy broth filled with mushrooms and rice.

"Sorry, I'm a terrible host. I forgot you hadn't eaten in a while." He cut the bread in half and loaded one side with butter before handing it over.

Kody took the bread and tried to clear her mouth before speaking. "It's fine. I was just thirsty before. I don't think I could have eaten until I cooled off and drank water." She ripped a chunk of bread off and dunked it in her soup before shoving it into her mouth. "Oh gawd. Is soo goowd."

Tristan grinned and dug into his own food. Kody watched him while he ate. Something about his smile made her heart bubble up in her chest, and she didn't think it was just the attraction to him she was trying to ignore. When Tristan smiled, the expression seemed uncomfortable on his face like he didn't do it often. It made her want to make him smile more, and maybe see if he could get used to it. He puzzled her, not at all what she expected.

When her stomach stretched to capacity, Kody eyed a few last roasted potatoes on her plate. She speared one with her fork. She could eat past the pain. It would be worth it for another bite. But the thought of lifting it to her mouth made her stomach cry, so she set it down and leaned back. Maybe she would wait a few minutes, let things digest, then she could finish the tray.

Her change in posture must have been a signal to Tristan, for he set down his tea and met her eyes. "I think we should head out in a week."

Kody blinked, more ready for a nap than to figure out what he was talking about. "Go where?"

"To the forest. A week would give us time to do a little research. I know a few people I could ask for gossip about the Elv, and it would give us time to prepare supplies for a trek."

"Are you sure you're okay leaving? I don't want to take you on a wild goose chase on my account. I could go on my own, or just not go at all."

Tristan shook his head. "This is too important. You need to find out who you have left, see if you have a home to return to. Most of us didn't have that option, but you do."

"And what if there's no one there?"

"There'll be someone. Maybe not family, but someone who knows your story, knows where you came from. Isn't that enough of a reason to go? You don't have to stay, but wouldn't it be nice to know your own story?"

Kody didn't reply. It would be nice. It was something she'd always wanted, but . . . "What if they're weird?"

Tristan snorted. "The Elv as a whole? Well, they probably will be. There's always culture shock, isn't there? But you're gonna get that whether you stay here or go there. Look, I haven't taken a vacation in two years. This will be fun."

"Well, I guess I need you either way. I don't speak the same language as anyone else."

Tristan sighed. "There are spells for teaching people languages, but they're expensive. I got one when I was six and the magical university scooped me up to test if I had magic."

"You grew up in a magical university?" Kody grinned, thinking of something with moving staircases and talking portraits.

"No, I don't have any magic. But I had to understand the examiners for them to be sure, so I got my languages for free. Some of the others had to learn the old-fashioned way. I have a—an acquaintance who's an Enchanter. I will see if he knows the spells and can send one."

"And until then?"

Tristan nodded. "Until then, I have a few projects I need to finish. I can show you around town a little, and we can figure out what to pack for our trip. Sound good?"

Kody nodded. And then, because she was a masochist, she ate another potato.

Tristan's neighbor stopped by to provide more clothes for Kody, and Kody was, for once, relieved she didn't speak the same language. The woman was cute, maybe a few years older than her, with golden brown skin and tight black curls. She had a bundle of clothes, all airy and light, but in colors brighter than Kody usually wore, and nothing with long sleeves. Kody fascinated the woman. She kept grabbing Kody's arm and trying to trace a swirl before Tristan would say something Kody didn't understand. She talked nonstop, asking her things and gesturing for Tristan to interpret. Did she have magic? Could she make plants grow? Finally, Tristan stopped translating and fielded all the questions himself, which Kody appreciated.

While thankful for the clothing, the neighbor's presence taught Kody one thing. She had absolutely no desire to meet anyone else who would marvel over her green skin and oddly shaped ears.

For the next three days, Kody didn't leave the apartment. She woke each morning to an empty apartment and a cold breakfast waiting for her. Tristan would meet her for lunch, then return in the early afternoon when it grew too hot to work. In the evenings, they played card games and Tristan tried to teach her a few words in what he called the common language, or he told her everything he knew of the Elvman, which wasn't much. He'd asked around about sightings of Elv over the years but hadn't gotten any great leads. Their plan, for now, was to enter the forest and travel north.

The desk drawer glowed several times a night, but Tristan never answered. Kody, antsy from isolation, wanted so badly to know who was on the other end and what they wanted that she nearly answered the calls herself, but then she remembered her lack of makeup and the obvious green swirls and left the orb in the drawer.

When language and history lessons grew dull, Kody tried to get Tristan to talk more about his own story, but it was like pulling nails.

She tried again during a game of rummy using cards Tristan

had bought and modified to match what Kody knew from Earth. She pressed him when it seemed like he was close to winning and being annoyingly smug.

"So do you like being a blacksmith?" Kody discarded to end her turn.

"Yes." Tristan snatched up her discard and grinned.

Kody rolled her eyes at his one-word answer. "What do you like about it?" He gave her a sharp look, as if trying to dissuade her from talking. Did he expect her to sit in silence or something? "Oh let me guess, you like the fire bit, don't you?" she asked.

He rolled his eyes and discarded a card she didn't need. "I like making something out of nothing."

Wow. That was a bit deeper than she expected, but from experience, drawing attention to it would just make him frown and clam up. Kody drew from the stock, getting a card Tristan needed, but she didn't. She held onto it and discarded a king. "So like, turning an iron lump into nails and horseshoes?"

"Sure." Tristan pulled from the stock and laid down four aces.

Kody ground her teeth. "What about more complex things? Like maybe an engine?"

Tristan looked up sharply, his eyes narrowing to slits when they met hers. "Been snooping, have you?"

Kody rolled her eyes and drew a new card. What else did he expect her to do all day? She could only play solitaire so often. "Come on, it's not like I understood anything. I majored in business." She finished her turn before pressing further. "So how would it work, exactly? Would you mine for fossil fuels in this world or something?"

"No need when magic is a free renewal resource." Tristan picked up her discard again, and she was sure he was close to winning.

"I thought you didn't know magic." Kody rearranged the cards in her hand and picked up Tristan's discard and started laying down her matches, so she wasn't caught with them at the end of the game.

"I don't," he said, his chin resting on his hand as he watched her unload her hand.

"Oh, is that friend of yours able to help with that part, then?" She shot an obvious glance at the desk drawer, currently pulsing with an unanswered call on the orb hidden within.

Tristan made a face as if the idea was unpleasant, but he didn't respond. He was the only person she'd seen for three days, and he couldn't even hold a proper conversation. It made her want to lash out. "Or is working with others a little too group project for you?" she asked.

"What is that supposed to mean?"

"Nothing."

"Whatever," Tristan muttered and laid down all the matched cards in his hand, going out. Then he left the table.

Kody sighed and tallied his win and her losses on their running score paper.

On her fourth day trapped in Tristan's apartment, Kody was well past stir crazy. She wandered from window to window, watching the traffic below. The people on the streets all wore bright colors like the ones she now owned, but now and then she spotted someone in a long cloak, hood pulled up over their heads, shading their faces from the sun. Finally, she wandered to Tristan's coat rack and ran a hand over the lining of his cloak. It would be warm, and maybe a little too long on her, but it would work. She found her shoes and draped the cloak over her shoulders.

Her heart beat a little faster as she descended the staircase, but she didn't let herself rethink her choice as she stepped out into the late morning sunlight. She was still in the discovery phase of her plan. Find out how this world worked and choose where she wanted to start her future. She could make a life here in Tristan's town, working at the tavern Tristan always went on about and being an openly Elvwoman living in a Hu city, but before she could commit to that path, she needed to give the Elvman life a chance. Once Tristan finished his pending work they could start on that journey.

She found Tristan's forge easily. The guide she met on her first day in the village, Peet, sat on a stool in the doorway, chatting along while Tristan struck a piece of metal with a large hammer. It took them a moment to notice her, and Peet smiled and waved before saying something to Tristan.

Tristan raised his eyebrows at her but didn't say anything or miss a beat while striking his hammer.

"We talked about me needing proper boots for our trip, and you taught me the word for it, so maybe I can manage," Kody said.

Tristan clanged his hammer a half dozen more times before setting it down and shoving the metal rod back into the fire. He breathed heavily, sweat dripping down his bare chest, and Kody tried not to notice how his muscles flexed when he took a deep drink of water. He turned to her, slightly out of breath.

"If you're up for it, Peet will go with you. He can make sure you don't get swindled."

Kody nodded, and Tristan turned to Peet. They spoke for a short time, Peet grinning and nodding to Kody enthusiastically. Tristan turned back to her. "I told him you should also get a cloak that fits you, and a few long sleeve shirts for the forest." Kody grinned, but Tristan rolled his eyes. "It's pointless to cover up all the time, but it will protect against bugs and some scrapes." Tristan dug around in a drawer and pulled out a small pouch that clinked when he tossed it to Peet. "Have fun."

"Ah! Fun!" Peet said to Kody in English and grinned, gesturing for her to follow. Tristan gave her a last nod before pulling out his red hot metal and picking up his hammer once again.

Peet chatted as they went, and Kody, at first tense and on edge, drifted into a relaxed mood. No one watched them pass or stopped and stared. With Peet at her side, Kody felt a sort of confidence, knowing he would engage anyone necessary, and she could stand by, hood low, and enjoy the afternoon.

The boot seller saw her face, and his stare was obvious, but not intrusive. Peet chatted with him until he relaxed and sold them a pair of worn caramel-colored leather boots that hit just below Kody's knees. She didn't relish lacing them every time she put them on, but they were so cute and fit an aesthetic she'd never have pulled off on the streets of Pittsburgh.

The seamstress also saw her swirls. They were impossible to hide as she measured Kody and handed over long-sleeved shirts in more muted colors Kody had picked. She had obvious shock at the sight of Kody but didn't treat her differently, and she seemed enthralled with Peet's conversation. Kody began to think maybe life in this town wouldn't be so bad. She could handle a few looks and curiosity. It was just another part of her life now.

Kody picked out browns and neutrals for her shirts, but the seamstress insisted on throwing in a few greens, for reasons Kody didn't want to think about. Her new cloak was mahogany and lightweight, with simple embroidery along the edge.

With their tasks complete, Peet led Kody to a spot in the market where the divine smells of varying foods wafted until her stomach growled. They ate seasoned meat on skewers, roasted nuts, something close to french fries smothered in a cheesy white sauce, and buns filled with jam. Kody tucked four extra buns in her pockets to share with Tristan later, in hopes of eliciting one of his grins.

They wandered the rest of the market, Peet pointing out odd or beautiful things as he chattered away. Kody didn't understand more than a word like good or bad, but she enjoyed herself all the same. She was looking through pretty scarves, dyed in ornate patterns, just to look, not to shop, when she picked out a few words from Tristan's language lessons, "Elv" and "woman" from a nearby conversation. She glanced over and saw two men in uniform. Her guard went up, and she pulled her hood lower over her face. The men weren't looking at her or gesturing in her direction. They didn't seem to notice her at all, but still they repeated those words. She found Peet and pulled him away until he understood she wanted to leave. If people were already talking about her, spreading rumors of an Elv woman in the city, would her presence really go overlooked for long?

Chapter Eight

"It's not that big of a deal," Tristan said, as he washed up in the bathroom while Kody recounted her day in the market. "Yeah, there's going to be talk and gossip, but the only way to avoid that is to live with the other Elv."

Kody deflated at his words. "So that's it? My answer is to go back to my people?"

Tristan sighed and looked at her. "Come on. It's not like that." He moved to the bedroom and dug around in a drawer for clean clothes. "The Hu don't hate the Elv. They're just curious. If you stayed here and lived here, that would be fine too. Once people get used to seeing you around, the looks will stop."

"Okay, so go back to my people or live as a sideshow freak. Got it." Kody left the bedroom so he could change, and flopped back on the couch, talking loud enough for him to hear. "How is this world better than Earth?"

Tristan took a long time to respond. He moved to the door-frame of the bedroom, wearing a deep blue shirt and tan pants that fit his muscular frame to perfection. He fiddled with the collar of the shirt as he met her eyes. "I never said it was better. I only said it was home."

Kody rolled her eyes. Oh no, she wasn't letting Tristan in a tight shirt sway her into a more biddable mood. "Right. Because you definitely seem at home here. You have what, one friend and a host of people calling you on your crystal ball that you never answer?"

Tristan shot Kody a glare that made her stomach tie in knots, and he disappeared back into the bedroom.

Kody busied herself with opening her new clothes. Tristan wanted to take her to a tavern for dinner and a show, or a 'tale' as he was calling it. He said story tellers projected a psychic image into the minds of those listening, like a magical stage performance or mental movie. Apparently, it was a great way to make money if you had the skill. It didn't take magic or anything, just someone really good at focusing their thoughts. Kody was more than interested, but she worried about how others would respond to her.

While she'd been out with Peet, she saw a woman selling cosmetics and was so tempted to buy foundation to cover her now brighter swirls. But the other part of her, a smaller but passionate part, didn't want to hide anymore. That part didn't want to sweat in long sleeves in the middle of a heat wave, and just wanted to be confident enough to live her life without fear or shame of being different. And now here she was, taking her anxiety out on Tristan and trying to get him to cancel the outing altogether.

The bedroom door opened, and Tristan appeared. "Do you need anything in the bathroom? I'm gonna take a shower."

"No, I'm okay." She didn't ask why he'd change if he was just gonna shower. In the tiny apartment, a shower was the easiest excuse for privacy, and she didn't blame him for wanting to avoid her.

Tristan nodded and disappeared into the bathroom. Kody tucked her new clothes away in a bedroom drawer and snatched the deck of cards off the desk and set up a game of solitaire at the kitchen table. Kody longed for books in English or even a way to charge her phone and read the dozens of books already downloaded. She didn't care that she'd read them before. She would happily reread the same book fifty times if only it provided something to occupy her mind.

Tristan emerged from the steaming bathroom and caught her rifling through her discard pile looking for the three of hearts, determined not to lose another game. He deposited his clothes in the bedroom and sat across from her.

Kody gathered up the cards and shuffled. "You know solitaire is only fun when you can get the computer to deal for you." She glanced up and met his caramel eyes, framed with the wet strands of his hair. His eyes were still dark and broody, but the edge of his mouth turned up in the slight smirk she was growing used to.

"It's not so tedious when you're good enough to win a hand."

Kody glared at him and started dealing rummy. "Not all hands are winnable, you know."

Tristan picked up his cards and rearranged them in his hand. "With how many games you've attempted the last few days, the statistics on unwinnable hands must be high."

Kody ground her teeth and flipped the top card off the stack. Tristan picked it up, and the game commenced. She won. Then he won twice.

They played a dozen hands before it was time for dinner. Kody checked the paper where they kept track of their wins. She was still up by a dozen points and smiled smugly while she grabbed her new cloak and Tristan ushered her out the door.

The Snarled Cello was a large tavern on the bottom floor of the Inn, with several floors of rentable rooms above. Kody tugged her hood up as they entered the large, boisterous dining room. Tristan maneuvered around the cramped, heavy wooden tables and chairs toward a table along the back wall. Kody kept her head low and her face covered though no one in the crowded room even glanced in their direction. She was bombarded by people laughing and talking with friends across the room. As they sat, she watched kids serve platters of roasted meats and vegetables or bowls of rice covered in thick stew. Everything was delicious and she relaxed into her chair.

A tall owl faced man with gray hair and a stern frown ambled over to their table and clapped Tristan on the shoulder. Tristan seemed to buckle under the blow but smiled up at the old man and gestured to Kody. She heard her name but understood nothing else he said.

The man seemed to frown down at her with the disappointment of a thousand school principals and said something in a booming voice she felt in her chest.

"He says you are very welcome here," Tristan translated.

Kody shot him a look. "No, he didn't."

Tristan laughed and after the man shot a stern look at him, he translated.

The man glared at Kody again, his big caterpillar eyebrows raising with interest, then he turned and stalked away, moving well between the packed tables.

Tristan chuckled again. "That's Graham. I told you about him."

Kody let out a small snort of shock. "*That* was the kind, caring man who takes in homeless kids and teaches them a trade so they can find jobs and provide for themselves?"

Tristan laughed again and nodded before taking a sip of his tea.

"What did he really say?"

Tristan rolled his eyes. "I told him you were one of the new Misplaced, freshly arrived, and he said 'Bah, another one? Well, you are very welcome here, child.'" Tristan said this in a deep aggressive voice and a scowl that totally mirrored the tavern owner. He laughed again. "He's a good man, but he can take some getting used to."

Kody frowned and watched the man as he moved around the tavern, greeting people and glaring at everyone he spoke to. "I think I had a substitute teacher like that once."

As the evening grew late, empty plates were cleared, mugs and cups were refilled, and more and more people made their way to the tavern, filling every chair, perching on tables, and standing in the back. When the room looked near ready to burst, Graham stood at the front and spoke. Tristan interpreted, scooting his chair closer to Kody so he could whisper in her ear.

"He says there are two tellers tonight, so we should get about four tales or so, unless there are encores."

A tall woman with blond hair and a cotton burgundy dress stood at Graham's gesture and stepped onto the stage. The crowd cheered.

"Remember, relax your mind, don't fight the vision," Tristan said before the woman raised her hands and spoke. "Gather in close, and I'll tell you the tale," Tristan interpreted.

It was as if someone had flipped a light switch, but instead of being overwhelmed by darkness, she was seeing a castle with ornate wooden columns and a handsome man with armor striding up the steps. Kody blinked a few times, but the image didn't clear. Somewhere she felt Tristan lean closer to her, felt the warmth of his body as his chest pressed into her arm.

"Before Kallen 'The Foolish' was known for his mistakes, he was known as Sir Kallen of Koom," Tristan whispered into her ear.

Kody shivered in the warm tavern air and relaxed into the story as Tristan narrated the life of a man who wanted to be a hero, but ended up getting his family slain. The tale was suspenseful and tragic. Kody wasn't the sort of person to cry at a movie, but there was something more real about this tale than any movie she'd seen. She felt for this man and the loss of everything he had, and at the end, she tried to subtly wipe a tear from her eye. The next tale was a love story that left her heart racing while Tristan whispered the details in his smooth voice. The third tale . . . It was Casablanca, like the actual movie. Tristan laughed at her shock and explained that some of the Misplaced often told tales in exchange for what they needed to get by, and once someone heard a tale, they could always retell it to others. "Kirk has told probably every major blockbuster from the last twenty years on Earth."

Kody snorted and leaned against Tristan's chest while he translated the lines, even though she had a general idea of the story.

They got seven tales that night, and two were movies she'd seen, while another was one of her favorite books. By the time the evening grew to a close and the crowd filed out to their homes or rented rooms, Kody felt relaxed and content. For a moment, she could imagine her life like this. Learning to read and speak the common language and listening to little pieces of her old life in tales a few times a week. Quiet evenings with Tristan, reading or playing other board games they could reinvent from their lives on Earth.

Her chest was full to bursting as they stepped out onto the dark street and Tristan led them back to his apartment. She didn't want to lose this peace, but she also needed to be realistic. Sure, she and Tristan had gotten cozy back in the tavern, but maybe it was a fluke. He hadn't been sending any obvious signals he was into her, and with her breakup with Roger so recent, she didn't want to deceive herself into crushing on a guy who just saw her as a friend or someone he had a duty to help.

The humidity still hung over the city in the late hour. They turned from a well-lit street onto one with fewer light globes illuminating the path, and Kody pulled back her hood, lifting her hair and letting what cool air there was hit the back of her neck. A green light appeared at the end of the road, and it caught Kody's eye. Most light globes she'd seen ranged from blue to white, but none so brilliantly green.

The light grew brighter for a moment, hovering chest high over the road, and moved. Kody blinked. Not just a light. A hand, glowing green under the light. A hand that connected to a figure in a dark cloak holding the light out before them. They turned toward Tristan and Kody. Tristan stopped and put a hand on her arm. As the person drew closer, Tristan pulled Kody back into the doorway of a dark building and stood in front of her. Kody's heart raced as she pulled her hood back up and tried to melt into the shadows while still peering over Tristan's shoulder.

The light grew closer and Kody could just make out the shape of a shorter person illuminated in the green glow under the long, flowing cloak. The person paused before their hiding space. Slowly, the stranger turned toward Kody and Tristan, and Kody could just see the lines of a soft feminine face, lit with green. The woman squinted into the dark before her and lifted the light. It grew brighter and brighter until its glow reached Tristan and Kody, and the woman grinned with triumph.

She spoke, and Kody, of course, understood nothing.

Tristan paused for a moment longer than Kody would have thought. The woman clearly saw them. Then at last he stepped forward and spoke. They exchanged a few words before the woman reached for Kody. Tristan blocked her, and she growled at him.

"What's happening?" Kody asked, frustrated at her ignorance.

Tristan said something else to the woman, and in response, she pulled off her hood. She was beautiful, and about the same age as Kody. Her features were soft and somehow familiar, her large eyes and a wide nose that fit her pouty lips and rounded cheeks perfectly. But the most stunning bit about her were the brilliant green swirls streaked across her dark complexion, glowing gently, not in the light she carried, but with their own glow of power.

"Is she an Elv?" Kody asked breathlessly.

Tristan met her eyes and nodded. "She's looking for her sister."

Chapter Nine

Something caught in Kody's throat. No, that wouldn't do. She would not cry on this street just because some glowing green girl claimed to be her long-lost family. She dug her nails into her thigh, trying to distract herself from the rush of emotions.

The woman locked her eyes on Kody and didn't look away. She spoke again.

Tristan looked at Kody, then back at the woman. The woman sighed and rolled her eyes. Such a relatable expression it caught Kody off guard. The woman clapped her hands together and the green light went out. A moment later, the swirls on her skin also stopped glowing. She opened her cloak revealing a pack and pulled out a small flower and held it out to Kody. It was hard to see in the dark alley, but it looked kind of like a lily or a trumpet flower.

"What's it for?" Kody asked.

"I think it's a language spell," Tristan said. "They are usually in flowers. You inhale, like smelling the flower, and it kinda downloads whatever language into your head. That's what I've been hoping Allen would send us."

Tristan said something to the woman again, and she nodded, then gestured to Kody.

"Yeah, it's a language flower, but she wants to see your face before giving it to you. In case her spell was leading her behind you and not actually to you."

"Should I do it?"

"That's up to you."

Kody let out a deep breath. She gingerly lowered her hood, and the woman stepped forward. She lifted her hand and another small green light exploded from her fingertips and floated into the space between them. This time it was brighter and a lighter green, almost white. It illuminated the street. The woman's stern face broke into a fierce smile, something glistening in the corners of her eyes, and she handed Kody the flower. Kody took it and looked down into the bloom, but it seemed like a completely normal flower.

The woman mimed lifting it to her face and taking a deep breath. Kody glanced at Tristan. "I think it's safe," he said.

Kody wasn't reassured, but she couldn't just stand out here all night staring at a flower. She wasn't sure she wanted a long-lost family and all the emotional baggage it included, but she also didn't want to be so afraid of disappointment that she missed out on something amazing.

Kody lifted the flower to her nose and took a deep breath.

She wasn't quite sure what happened next, but when Kody did again have a grasp on the world, her head felt like it was splitting in two, and she was very aware Tristan had his arms wrapped tightly around her, holding her up.

"She's coming to. See? She's fine," a woman said in a firm yet silky voice.

"How many languages did you load on that thing?" Tristan said, his voice rumbling through Kody's back.

Kody tried opening her eyes and winced.

"The headache will pass in a minute. Just breathe through it," Tristan said.

"Let me help her. I can soothe the ache," the woman said.

"Just give her space."

Kody found her feet and pushed Tristan away. Her stomach was turning, and her head buzzed like it was knitting itself back together. She kept a hand on Tristan's arm and bent over, breathing deeply.

"I'm sorry, dear sister. I forgot these things usually take better in the young. I should have told the maker not to add the classic languages for now."

Kody slowly straightened and opened her eyes. Everything before her swam like she was underwater.

"Classics? Seriously, what were you thinking? You're lucky her brain isn't dripping out of her ear."

Kody knew now why the woman's features looked so familiar. They were like her own. The same nose, same eyes, but where her sister was short, her face round, Kody was tall, her face longer and her features sharper.

"Quiet. I don't need a Hu telling me how to treat my sister. Her Elv heritage is strong. She is not some frail thing."

For the first time since coming to this world, Kody truly and completely believed all of this was real. She had absolute confidence this was her world, and she would never leave it.

"You realize your sister is half Hu, right? You might want to curb that prejudice a little."

Her confidence and conviction only lasted a moment before the doubt this was all a delusion crept back in, but she ignored it.

"She is Hu, and she is Elv, and she is perfect. I have no prejudice against the Hu, I am only very aware of the lacking your culture brings to your spirit."

It was strange. As her head cleared, Kody could make out the individual words the woman, her sister, and Tristan said, and she knew the words were wrong, not English, but somehow she understood everything perfectly.

Tristan put a hand on Kody's shoulder. "Are you back with us now?"

Kody blinked at him. "I think so." The words felt wrong in her mouth, but Tristan just nodded, understanding the language her brain had picked in reply. Kody turned to the woman. "Um, thank you for the language. I've felt isolated not understanding anyone but Tristan since I got here."

The woman nodded. "It is my honor." She glanced at Tristan, then back at Kody. "I'm glad you found someone in this village you could converse with. The Hu do not always take kindly to our kind. But that no longer matters. I will take you home where you belong. Our father is eager to see you."

Kody took a deep breath, so many emotions coursing through her, but emotions didn't matter. She would stick to the plan and make a conscious, rational decision about which was the most practical place to live and start a life. "I want to see your home and meet everyone. Tristan was going to take me in a few days, but I'm not totally sure I want to live there permanently."

The woman frowned, and Kody tensed, sure she was going to say something harsh, or reject her, but then after a moment, her face relaxed.

"I understand. You don't know us. This boy, though he is Hu, he came from your world, so there is understanding and familiarity. Take your time, get to know me and our people. We are Elv. Time is something we have plenty of." She said this last part with a grin, like it was some kind of inside joke, and Kody found herself wanting to know everything she could about this woman.

"Thank you," Kody said. "Um, do you have a place to stay tonight?"

The woman opened her mouth, but before she spoke, Tristan cut in. "If not, you can stay with us. My apartment is small, but you can bunk with Kody." He nodded to Kody. "If that's okay. I can even sleep in my forge and give you the whole flat if that's easier."

Kody rolled her eyes. "We aren't kicking you out of your apartment. We'll make it work."

The woman smiled and nodded to Tristan. "Thank you. I would be happy for a place to stay." She turned to Kody and took her hand. "You are known as Kody?"

Kody nodded, not sure what to say. The woman smiled warmly. "I am Briony."

"That's lovely. It's wonderful to meet you, Briony. This is Tristan."

Briony glanced at Tristan, then looked back at Kody. "I cannot express how glad I am to know you. In the morning, we can set forth on our journey and I can tell you all the family stories."

"Oh, Tristan and I still needed some supplies before we set out."

"Don't worry, I can provide for the both of us in the forest," Briony said.

"But Tristan is coming too, aren't you?" Kody turned from her sister and met Tristan's eyes.

His eyebrows went up, and he glanced at Briony. "Well, I was planning to, but now you have a much better guide."

"Oh, you still have to come. We've talked so much about what we will find in the forest, it wouldn't feel complete if you weren't there," Kody said with a grin, as if it was a joke, but really she was screaming inside. It wasn't that she didn't feel safe traveling with Briony, it was that she so dearly wanted a buffer between herself and the past her sister brought with her. And a large part of her didn't want to part ways with Tristan, as if leaving him would mean the end of whatever existed between them, budding friendship or any possibility of more.

After a long pause, Briony spoke. "You are welcome to join us if it will bring my sister comfort. It's not unprecedented for Hu to venture into our city, but you will be asked to keep your experiences of our city to yourself."

Tristan nodded. "I can do that." Kody rolled her eyes. Tristan excelled at keeping things to himself.

"Fine. We'll plan and prepare tomorrow, and leave the following morning," Briony said.

They all agreed, and Tristan led them the rest of the way to his apartment.

After they settled into bed, Kody lay on her side staring into the darkness as she tried to force her mind to still and drift into sleep. Her whole body buzzed with the revelation of the evening and sleep felt an eternity away. Briony was happy to share Tristan's wide bed with Kody. Kody was only a little uncomfortable with the thought, but it wasn't about the bed, it was about letting someone into her life who had the potential to hurt her deeper than any romantic fling ever could. She had worked so very hard to convince herself a biological family would never happen for her, and here she was now, lying next to a sister who was so very different in almost every way and yet felt oh so familiar.

While they had readied for bed, Briony commented on how odd the shower and bath combo was. She mentioned something about a waterfall and a natural pool, but Kody just couldn't picture anything other than an old shampoo commercial. She absolutely couldn't imagine the magical forest kingdom her sister described. To think in two days they would reenter the strange forest Kody had first arrived in and start a trek to a magical Elvman city to meet her biological family. The thoughts sent alternating jets of excitement and anxiety coursing down her body. Briony hadn't understood her apprehension. To her, Kody was going home, and that was the obvious option. Kody couldn't explain her fears and worries without opening up more than she was comfortable.

At long last, Kody's mind sank and drifted toward peaceful oblivion, but just before she faded to dreamland, she heard her sister whisper in the dark next to her.

"I am so happy to know you at last, Kody, my sister. I will take you home to our father and our family will be whole. Just you wait and see."

Chapter Ten

Planning and preparing the next day turned out to mean Tristan and Kody showing Briony their supplies and Briony telling them basically everything was pointless. They didn't need a tent or heavy hiking gear or the sharp blades Tristan insisted they would need to cut through the foliage. The medical supplies and their camping and cooking instruments would be redundant.

"The forest isn't such an inhospitable place as you seem to think," Briony told Tristan as he showed her a bottle of magical bug spray.

"Really?" Kody asked, rolling her eyes. "Someone should have told the forest that on my first trip through."

"Yeah, your blessed forest chewed Kody up and spit her out." Tristan threw his bug spray into the "staying" pile. "My medicines are the only reason she didn't lose a leg."

"What?" Kody gasped. "You didn't tell me that."

Tristan shrugged. "I didn't wanna freak you out, but the poisoned gash on your leg was deep. Left untreated, it could've been bad."

Briony paused in repacking Kody's bag and sat back on her heels. "That surprises me. Maybe the forest didn't want you to leave once it had found you again." She shrugged and resumed packing. "Regardless, you will be welcome with me." She shot a glance at Tristan. "You too, I suppose."

"Well, that fills me with cheer," Tristan said and stood. "I've got a few things to clean up in the forge. Meet me there in an hour and we can head to the market to get our provisions."

Tristan left and Kody fiddled with the discarded medical supplies while Briony continued sorting Kody's pack. She'd removed everything with long sleeves for their journey, saying it was too hot and they would provide Kody everything she needed when the weather changed.

"Is the forest really alive?" Kody asked.

"Of course," Briony said immediately. Then she grinned and shot Kody a playful look. "It depends a little on what you mean by alive. Every tree, shrub and moss is alive, a separate organism in the biosphere of the forest. But is it sentient?" Briony shrugged. "Some think so. Dad says it is. It told him when you arrived."

Dad. Both Kody's and Briony's dad. It was such an odd thought, such a heavy title, yet used so freely. Kody ignored it. "But how would that even work? You just said they are all separate plants. How could the forest be a sentient being?"

Briony sat back on her heels again and frowned. "Well, I've never studied biological agency or anything of the sort, but it could be some type of hive mind, or a single element in the environment." She folded a yellow top while she spoke, and finally shrugged, placing it back in Kody's pack and moving on. "Maybe it's our great creator god using the forest as their hands. It doesn't really matter if it's sentient or not. It feels alive, and it has its own sort of magic. Like magic calls to like, and it responds to its people in kind. The same magic that runs through you lives in that forest. You'll feel it. You'll see."

"Briony, I don't have any magic."

"Of course you do. You're an Elv."

"Half Elv though."

"Still an Elv."

"Yeah, but what if I'm not Elv enough? Maybe I didn't get any of the magic and that's why the forest didn't like me?"

Briony put the last garment in the pack and went to the couch and sat next to Kody. She put a hand on Kody's arm. Kody tried not to stiffen. "I know I gave your Tristan grief over it earlier, but the Elv don't hate Hu."

"He's not my anything," Kody muttered.

Briony continued, as if not hearing her. "Your mother, our father's first queen, was Hu, and everyone in the forest dearly loved her."

"You knew her?"

"Goodness no. She passed only a few years after your disappearance, a hundred or more years ago, from grief, our father always said. I'm not nearly so old." Briony's hand tightened on Kody's shoulder.

Kody nodded. There was no need to mourn a woman so far out of reach, yet her chest still throbbed with the missed opportunity.

"I forgot about the time difference between our worlds," Kody said at last. "You're what, maybe twenty or twenty-two?"

"I'm thirty-seven, actually."

"What?" Kody exclaimed a little loudly.

Briony chuckled. "Elv age much slower than Hu once we reach maturity. Just wait. You're there now. You won't show any more signs of aging for at least fifty years."

Kody blinked and looked away. She'd left Earth just in time, it would seem. How long would she have lasted before people noticed she didn't match the age on her ID? She would have been fine for ten years maybe, but twenty? Thirty?

They finished the last of the packing that they could do before shopping and cleaned up before donning cloaks and heading down to the forge.

They met up with a surprisingly clean Tristan whose work for the day clearly hadn't been intense, and headed to the market to grab extra food and trail snacks for the trip. Tristan offered to go by himself, thinking Briony might be as uncomfortable as Kody traveling through the town, but she was not. She was curious to explore and wander among the Hu. Kody pulled her hood lower over her face while Briony smiled and pointed out interesting things, laughing and trying to pull Kody into conversations.

While Briony was distracted by a pair of soft leather boots, Tristan pulled Kody aside and held out a small, bundled handkerchief.

"What is it?"

Tristan dragged open the edges of the handkerchief to reveal something delicate and shiny. "I figured before you set out tomorrow to find your new home, you needed something to remember your old one."

He pulled out a chain with a small silver pendant on the end. Kody took it carefully and examined it, trying to understand what it was. "It looks like a bridge," she said, hoping she wasn't wrong.

Tristan gave her a weak grin and scratched the back of his head. "The city of bridges; it's the only thing I remember about Pittsburgh." At Kody's stunned expression, he grimaced. "That's right, isn't it? I can make something else if it's wrong."

"No, no, that's perfect. Better than some sports logo." Kody smiled and fiddled with the clasp.

"Here, let me." Tristan took the necklace, unclasped it, and held it out.

Kody turned her back to him and pulled her curls away from her neck. Tristan's calloused fingers scraped against her skin as he draped the necklace.

"No matter what you find in the forest, your old life still made you the brilliant person you are now, and that shouldn't be forgotten."

Kody dropped her hair and fiddled with the pendant. "Thank you, it's perfect."

"I know," Tristan said, his eyes filled with something other than artistic pride as he met hers.

Kody felt her cheeks warm and turned to find Briony, still absorbed in a pair of knee-high boots, though not so distracted she didn't shoot Kody a sly grin when she joined her.

They needed little in the way of provisions, and their purchases were quickly finished, but still, Briony led Kody further into the market to see all they could find. Tristan followed dutifully. Briony marveled over a yellow dress made of gauzy fabric when two large forms loomed behind Kody.

"Honored guests," a deep voice said, causing Kody to jump. She spun to see two tall men in what she could only assume were soldier uniforms.

"We carry a message from our king," the bulkier of the two, a brown-eyed man with a light tanned complexion, said.

Tristan stepped up beside Kody, but Briony didn't bother turning as she stretched and examined the fabric of the dress.

"I don't need any message from your king. I'm busy shopping. Can't you see?" Briony said.

"My ladies, the king begs for you to see him," he said, addressing Kody and Briony both. "Please, grant us this request and return with us to the palace."

"What does the king want with them?" Tristan asked, crossing his arms and stepping in front of Kody.

"Our king has long wished to speak with the Elvman, to make peace. Please grant us this opportunity."

Kody traded looks with Tristan, who shrugged. Briony sighed and dropped the dress back on the rack.

"We will come with you to hear your king, but our time is limited," Briony said. She nodded to Kody reassuringly. "Sometimes being a princess means doing things you don't want to do for the sake of diplomacy," she told Kody with a weak smile.

The guards let them through the city and up a series of large hills that ended with a sight that caused Kody to stop in her tracks. A tall, perfect fairy-tale castle straight out of her wildest dreams appeared before them, stretching into the sky, and took Kody's breath away. No clunky towers or angles, every inch flowed in sweeping curves and sloped rooftops. Briony stopped next to her while the guards and Tristan continued on a ways before realizing the women had paused.

"Lovely isn't it?" Briony said with a wistful voice Kody hadn't heard from her before. "Our people built that castle."

"What?" Kody asked, glancing away from the castle for only a moment.

"Long ago, back when this continent was split between our people, the Dwarv, and the Avi, before the Hu invaded and committed genocide against our peoples, that castle was ruled by a great Elv king. Our family was always of the forest, but there are many royal lines among our people that no longer hold the land they once ruled."

Briony went quiet again and looked up at the castle as she took in a deep, slow breath. "I love that castle. It's the prettiest one still standing in all of Eres. When I was small, I always dreamed of stealing it back from the Hu." She glanced at Kody and smiled, nudging her sister in the ribs. "But of course that would be a diplomatic nightmare, right?"

Kody smiled back wearily, not sure if she was joking or not. They continued up the path and crossed under a brilliantly carved stone archway that somehow appeared as if many concrete vines had grown out of the ground and wound together to form a tunnel.

The castle was even lovelier up close. Made of some pale smooth rock, each stone forming the structure fit together so perfectly it was as if the castle was grown and not built, and every door and doorway had botanical themed carvings giving greater emphasis to the life and energy of the castle. The furniture and decorations they passed, paintings and tapestries, none of it felt like it matched the castle. As if the space was decorated by someone who didn't quite understand the design and intent of the hallways and rooms.

They were led to a large room with columns like tall old redwoods topped with beautiful vine-like arches holding up the high ceiling. When they entered, Briony lowered her hood and allowed it to fall back on her shoulders like a cape, uncovering her green swirled arms and her flowing lilac tunic below.

A myriad of people stood around the room and lined the edges, and they all hushed and turned at their entrance.

On the far side of the room sat a man Kody assumed was the king in a grand chair on top of a dais.

The king was . . . young. Maybe fifteen or sixteen, with a strong chin and clever eyes. When they entered, he excused himself from a conversation and rose. He left the dais and crossed the room until he stopped a few feet from Kody and her companions, the guards quietly disappearing into the background. Kody wasn't sure what to do. Tristan bowed, but Briony did not, so she decided on a brief nod that felt like a compromise between the two. To her great embarrassment, the king bowed deeply to Briony and her. Kody tipped back her hood as a slight concession, not wanting to seem rude by staying in shadow.

The king rose and placed a hand on his chest. "Thank you for accepting my invitation. I am Corinne, and it is my great pleasure to meet you."

He looked expectantly at Briony, and Kody also looked at Briony waiting for her lead.

"I know who you are," Briony said in a strong and somehow commanding tone. "Tell us for what reason you have waylaid us so that we may be on our way."

A slight murmur rose from those standing around the room,

but Kody didn't turn her head to look. She hoped her sister's rudeness didn't get Tristan into trouble somehow.

The king seemed to ponder her for a moment before speaking. "My family has always known of your people and your country bordering our own, my ancestors and particularly my father did not always take measures to foster a positive relationship with your people." He paused and Kody wondered what history she was missing. "This is something I wish to amend."

"Attempting to mend centuries of wrongs between our people is a tall order, indeed." Briony tilted her head. "One I hope not foolishly dreamt up by someone young and inexperienced."

The king bit his lip, frowning slightly, but to Kody's surprise, he didn't look frustrated or angry. "What task has brought you to my city that I may assist you with?"

"Nothing we need your help with, I assure you." Briony glanced at Kody. "I came to retrieve my sister and bring her back to my people. We leave in the morning."

The king focused his attention on Kody. "You and yours will always be welcome in my city, and I would never wish to delay your journey."

Kody wasn't sure what to say, so she half nodded again.

The king glanced at Tristan. "You are the Misplaced from Pundica, are you not? The one who studied with Blacksmith Rawford. Tristan of Pundica, yes?"

"Yes, Your Majesty. Although I have spent many more years in Rohap than I have lived in Pundica."

"I see. Then I will happily claim you as one of my people." The king smiled. It was a good-natured smile, as if he genuinely was happy to gain Tristan as a member of his country, and Kody decided she liked this young, informal king. "Tell me, how did you become host to our fine friends?"

Tristan glanced at Briony before speaking. "I met Kody shortly after she arrived from the illusion." The king's eyes snapped to Kody with renewed interest. "As you may be aware," Tristan continued, "since the Spell of the Misplaced was broken, some Misplaced have taken longer than others to return home. Being that I was the only one in Rohap who speaks the same language as Kody, I offered to help her back home."

"I was not aware the spell had affected the Elvman lines as well. Forgive me for my ignorance, your highnesses." He bowed again to Kody and Briony.

At his words, the people around the edges of the room stirred and their low voices became a buzzing in the background.

"Wizard Viclor's spell did not specify country names," Tristan explained. "It referenced a map of the continent."

"Oh I see," the king said. "An imprecise spell directed at the continent caused even those kings and queens hidden in plain sight to be so affected." He nodded to Briony. "I understand your anticipation of returning home with your sister. I'm sure your family has long since ached for her return. I will not delay you any longer, but I would ask a favor, if I may."

Briony seemed to think about this for a moment before nodding. "You may ask, though I cannot guarantee its fulfillment."

The king smiled and nodded slightly. "I asked that you would consider returning in the future after you and your sister have settled. Perhaps you can serve as an ambassador to your people and we can speak of diplomacy between our kinds to mend some of our centuries of wrongs."

Kody watched Briony carefully as her sister considered his request. "I will return one day and we can speak of diplomacy."

"And may I know what name to address you as, so I might tell my heirs in case you choose not to return in my lifetime?" he said with a grin, as if suspecting Briony might dawdle in her fulfillment of her promise.

Briony smirked slightly. "I am Briony, daughter of Callum, Princess of Hivagora. And my sister Kody, daughter of Callum, Princess of Hivagora. And though time sometimes becomes trivial to those of us who have much of it, I will try my best to return within your lifetime, for I think diplomacy with a sharp Hu might be an enjoyable pastime."

The king nodded. "I hope to live up to your expectations, Princess Briony." He turned to Tristan. "Tristan of Rohap, thank you for your time and for assisting our guests." He turned to Kody. "Princess Kody, may the road find you safely with your family once again."

"Thank you," Kody replied.

The king nodded to them all once again and turned, heading back to his dais, while Briony led Kody and Tristan from the throne room.

"Will you really return?" Kody asked her sister when they were once again outside of the castle.

"Of course," she said matter-of-factly. "How else could I ever expect to take this castle back for our people?" She smiled and Kody couldn't help but grin back, even though she still wasn't sure if she was serious or joking.

"He seemed a little young for marrying, if you ask me," Tristan said with a smirk. "Is that why you plan to wait a few years to return?"

Briony screwed up her face. "Gross. I wouldn't marry a Hu. There are other ways to get a castle. Besides, I already have a love."

"You do?" Kody asked.

"Yes. You will meet him on our return." Briony's face broke up into a pleased smile, as if her mind were suddenly far away.

"That's the real reason she wants to get on the road," Tristan whispered loudly enough for Briony to hear while he lightly elbowed Kody in the ribs. Briony didn't stop smiling, and Kody laughed and didn't even care when her hood fell to her back, delighting in the afternoon with Tristan and her sister.

They had a quiet evening, everything they needed for their journey packed up and waiting by the door. They joked about the afternoon at the castle and how Briony would redecorate when she was queen, and had fun teaching Briony how to play card games from Earth. It was enough fun to distract Kody from the anxiety creeping in at the thought of meeting her birth father. Callum, King of the Elvman.

Unfortunately, the distractions only lasted as long as the games, and as Kody turned off the light globe and lay down next to her sister to sleep, she couldn't help but worry she'd never be enough for the Elvman king.

Chapter Eleven

This trek through the forest was different for Kody. Paths seemed to open for them between the trees as if ushering them in, and through an entire day of traveling the forest, not once did Kody trip or stumble on a branch, root, or vine. As the sun dropped and the forest grew dim, they found themselves in a small clearing with a cold fire pit and beds of soft moss circling the perimeter, as if it was exactly where the forest wanted them.

Tristan walked around the perfect campsite and shot Briony a quizzical look. "Is this place for real?"

Briony grinned and dropped her pack. "Kody, help me gather some of this wood and we'll see if you have the gift to light a fire with your magic."

Something raced in Kody's chest, and she dropped her pack next to Briony's while Tristan pulled dinner things from his pack.

Along the tree line of their clearing was an ample amount of fallen and dried branches, just waiting for them to collect. Breaking some branches down, Briony showed Kody how to build a proper fire when she admitted she'd never built one. Building the fire was logical and easy; lighting it proved harder.

"Not every Elv has the ability to influence the ruakh around them," Briony said.

"Wait, what's ruakh?" Kody struggled a little with the odd pronunciation.

"Ruakh is the name for the magic flowing through our world. It's like the moisture hanging in the air after a rainstorm. It lives and moves in the world and only some can reach out and touch it."

"So I might not have magic after all?" Kody asked.

"No, you have magic—ruakh—flowing through you. All Elv do, but only some can influence it to perform what you think of as magic," Briony explained. "Elv come in two kinds, those who can perform magic and those with exceptionally long lives. All Elv have long lives, you understand, but those who can't touch and influence the ruakh, their lives are several times longer than the others of our people."

Tristan scooted closer and pulled an apple out of their bag. "So it's like using magic burns through their life faster?" he asked.

Briony shrugged. "Some would say so, but it's a long-debated topic. No one knows for sure, only that it is usually so."

"So I might do magic, or I might live a really long time?" Kody asked.

Briony nodded and handed Kody a small twig, about six inches long. "Now, creating fire is one of the most basic skills learned by those who can influence the ruakh. This stick is wood, and wood likes burning when it's dead and dry. It's a part of its nature to break down and return to the eres, and that can either happen naturally over time or through the reaction caused by fire."

Kody nodded and wiggled in her crisscross seated position on the moss. A looming pressure grew in her chest, a fear that she wouldn't be able to do this. Would her father, when she met him, care that she couldn't use magic? She didn't know what use her long life would be as it was. If she could do magic, maybe it would be easier to find a purpose, build a plan.

Briony picked up her own twig. "Ruakh flows around this stick just as it does around us, and if we ask it nicely, the ruakh will ignite this wood, reacting with its nature, and causing it to burn. It takes intent, will, and a focused mind." The green swirls over Briony's arms and face flashed with a green glow and the twig in Briony's hand sparked, a small flame blooming at its tip, growing steadily stronger as it burned down the length of wood.

Kody's heart raced at the obvious display of magic. She hoped she could do this. She needed to do this, to prove she was good enough, and also because it was freaking cool. Tristan's loud crunching of his apple next to her pulled her back to the present.

Kody wiggled again in her seat and held up the twig. "Okay, so what do I do?"

"Imagine the stick burning, focus on it, and then just push the image into the stick," Briony said simply as she glanced again at her own stick. Her swirls flared and the flame went out, smoke trickling from the scorched wood into the air above.

Kody nodded and stared at the twig. She focused on its color, a lighter brown than her own skin, and although the surrounding trees had green leaves, this stick was dead and dry, firm in her hand but also brittle. She imagined what that twig would look like with fire lapping at its edge and tried to push the thought out.

A fart nearly snuck out and she stopped and let out a deep breath.This wasn't working.

"Can't you just lay your hand on her shoulder or something and sense her magic?" Tristan asked.

Briony rolled her eyes. "I thought I already explained she has magic inside of her. I don't need to see the strength of her power, which is all that would tell me. I need to know if she has the skill to use it. It's like knowing if someone can wiggle their ears. I know she has ears, but can she wiggle them? We won't know until she tries."

Tristan shrugged and took another noisy bite of his apple.

Kody ignored their exchange and thought about when she first arrived in this forest. It had been so overwhelmingly different. The temperature, the lack of noise, the density of the ground, the weight of the air . . .

The air felt alive around her, and that was when her green swirls had glowed.

The weight of the air moving against her never really went away, but Kody learned to ignore the feeling of that otherness. She closed her eyes and felt for it now. There it was, not quite a presence, but a weight she'd never known during her life on Earth. She reached for it and found it responded, moving around her like smoke caught in an air current. Kody opened her eyes, and stared at the twig in her raised, green-glowing fist. She imagined the stick alight with fire, and somehow deep inside, she pushed with all her might and willed the surrounding magic to make it happen.

The stick exploded, shooting small shards of burning wood in every direction.

Everyone ducked and shielded themselves too late. Tristan cursed, and Briony sat up, laughing.

Kody rubbed at a spot on her cheek that'd been hit. The spot didn't hurt past the initial sting, but her fingers came away covered with soot, as if the wood had burned up too quickly to cause any damage. She turned to check on Tristan, who was grinning and brushing spots of soot off his shirt. He smiled at her and wiped a spot on her forehead with his thumb.

"Well, that answers that question," Briony said. Tristan dropped his hand and picked his apple back up, studying it for dirt or soot before taking another bite.

It didn't take long for Kody to figure out how to cause a flame to stay on a twig, and then to focus the magic on the right spots of the campfire to create an even and steady burn.

After a quick dinner, Kody sat on the moss against a log, watching the fire consuming the wood. She felt elated, like she could do anything. She'd never felt so powerful as she had after lighting the fire. Not powerful as in she wanted to control anyone or change the world, but powerful in herself, like she could make her own life, set her own path wherever she desired. If she'd ever felt like this, even for a day in her old life, she never would have let someone like Roger walk all over her.

A small fuzzy body scurried into Kody's line of sight and she jumped as the little creature came closer. "Awe, there's a little mouse," Kody announced. The first was quickly followed by a second, and she watched as they moved closer to the fire. "No, no little mousy," Kody said.

"Kody, it's okay, it's just—"

"It's gonna get burned!" She reached for the mice, trying to block them from the flame, but it was so hot she flinched. Just as the mice reached the flame, Briony had a hold of her arm and pulled her back from the fire.

"Dear one, relax and leave the cindix alone," Briony said.

"Why would they just walk into the fire like that?" Kody asked, a heavy weight in her chest.

Tristan burst out laughing behind Kody, and she glared at him. Didn't these people care at all for small creatures?

"Look again, dear sister," Briony said, pointing to the fire.

Kody grimaced, afraid of what she would see, but the mice weren't as she imagined them, shriveled and burnt in the fire. She scooted closer, and Briony kept a hand on her arm as if to prevent her from jumping to her own crispy end.

At the fire's base, two small fuzzy creatures moved. They were orange, or maybe a burnt orange, blending well with the fire, and while they looked like mice, they had cute fuzzy tails. As she watched, a third creature scurried into the fire and started chewing on the blackened wood.

"What are they?"

"Cindix. They eat ash. They usually survive on old burned trees and such, but their favorite is fresh burning ash," Briony said.

"We'll probably have a dozen in the fire by morning," Tristan said with a last chuckle.

"Wow." Kody sat back in her spot, this time watching the small creatures. She saw one licking the black burning wood with its tiny pink tongue, and it made her smile. There were so many wondrous things in this new world of hers, a part of her that still worried about getting back to Earth relaxed. She couldn't wait to see what new wonders she discovered tomorrow.

Eventually, they each found soft spots on the moss and curled up under their cloaks, plenty warm in the cooling summer air. Before she even got close to drifting off, Tristan spoke.

"Kody, do you know self-defense?"

She paused, not sure how to reply. "I know the basics."

"What are the basics?" he asked.

Kody blew out a deep breath. "Well, if someone tries to hurt you, aim for the soft bits. Kidney, nuts, and eyes."

She heard Briony snort, and when Tristan spoke again, she could tell he was grinning.

"That's fair, but not super practical."

"Why do you ask?"

"I was thinking, magic lessons are great and all but knowing some self-defense would be good too, you know?"

"What do I need to defend against exactly?"

"There are always things. It's better to know even if you don't need it," Tristan said.

"There's plenty of defensive magic I can teach you," Briony said. "It would be more effective than anything else. Not that you need it in our city, but it's still good to be prepared."

Kody shrugged and rolled onto her side, tired from the long day of walking and practicing magic for the first time. "I guess knowing both wouldn't hurt," she said, before drifting off to sleep.

Kody awoke to a rustling sound close to her head but didn't feel the need to open her eyes and investigate. She dozed again. What felt like a moment later, Kody felt something touch her arm and opened her eyes. Briony leaned over her, grinning.

"Mm. Do you need help finding the bathroom or something?"

Kody asked, trying to pull her cloak over her head, but Briony pulled the cloak down.

"Come, I want to show you something I think you will enjoy," Briony said, ripping Kody's cloak off with one quick tug. Kody curled into a little ball in protest, but it was no use. Reluctantly, she rose and sat on a log near the still warm embers of the fire where Briony was adding more logs. Kody spotted her cloak next to her sister and snatched it, wrapping it around herself, more for comfort than for warmth in the balmy morning air. Tristan rose and gave Kody a little good morning wave before moving toward the trees where their camp toilet was dug.

"Okay, now watch here in the ash," Briony said, tapping Kody's knee to get her attention. She pointed to the bottom of the campfire. It was a smooth surface where the ash had settled over the ground, but Briony used a stick and pointed to lumps and irregularities where Kody assumed half burned sticks or rocks hid under the ash. "Do you see it?"

Kody shook her head. "See what?"

"Just watch this spot here while I light it," Briony said as she pointed to a small lump of ash. The new logs caught fire and Kody leaned in. Did the lump move? Flames crawled up the fresh logs, and slowly the lump seemed to rise, then all at once it shook, and out popped a little sleepy cindix looking up at the flames, blinking its big eyes. All over the fire little cindix awoke out of the ashes and busied themselves with licking their paws and cleaning their small orange noses and ears.

"Ohmygosh! They're just so adorable!" Kody squealed, pulling the cloak tight around herself, overcome by the tiny, cute creatures.

Tristan set a kettle of water on the embers and chuckled. "So you're one of those girls who cries over baby kittens?"

"I don't know what you're trying to imply, but 'baby kittens' is redundant, and they are quite worth crying over, thank you very much."

Tristan rolled his eyes and offered her his hand. Kody looked at the hand—it was a very nice hand—and looked back at Tristan. "Can I help you with something?" she asked.

"Didn't we agree on self-defense training?" Tristan asked.

Kody shook her head. "Not before I get some of that caffeinated tea."

Briony snorted.

Tristan just wiggled his fingers.

Kody glanced back at the offered hand and groaned before taking it. Kody was on the tall side of average for a girl, and she'd always had larger hands and feet. Tristan's hand engulfed hers, wrapping around her palm and reaching for her wrist, he then pulled her to her feet in a powerful sweep that made her think about heavy hammers and blacksmith tools. It distracted her so much that she almost ended up in the fire. Or would have had Tristan not caught her, his hands now tight on her waist. She looked up into his caramel eyes, wondering if this would be their moment, and then Briony coughed.

"Are you steady?" Tristan asked.

Kody nodded but didn't try speaking. Tristan released her and stepped over her log seat into the open place where he'd slept. Kody took a deep breath to center herself and followed. The moss was soft under her bare feet, damp in some places from the morning dew, and warm in others, as if still reflecting the heat from Tristan's sleeping form.

"Okay, so yesterday you mentioned the basics," Tristan said.

"Right," Kody said, recalling the one-hour self-defense class all the girls in her foster home took when she was fifteen. "Aim for the soft bits. Kidney, eyes, and nuts."

Tristan grinned. "Yeah, great for the basics, but unfortunately, it's too basic. Every guy on any planet is raised from a young age to protect his—well you get it. Instead, I'm going to show you a few hand and wrist holds and how to break them. Your best line of defense is always to get away."

Kody nodded. That made sense. She wasn't fast, but she had long legs.

Over the next twenty minutes, Tristan showed her several ways to break someone's grip, standing way too close for her to concentrate half the time and switching holds too frequently for her to remember what to do.

When they reached a lull, Briony brought Kody a mug of strong tea and showed her a spell that could create a bubble of air between her and an attacker, throwing them off. Kody drank her tea and then tried the magic, but she couldn't quite figure it out. After a breakfast of oatmeal, they cleaned up, and Briony showed her how to magically put out the fire before they continued their journey.

By lunch, they reached a wide and lazy river. Trees grew dense all along the bank, casting the water in shadows, but their path opened perfectly to a small rocky beach. Briony knelt at the river's edge and dipped her hand in the water for a moment before rising. "We should take a break," she suggested.

Kody agreed, dropping her pack and pulling out lunch. As soon as she ate her food, Tristan reached down to pull her up, and it was back to breaking holds. She was just making progress when Briony cut in and had her try the bubble magic again.

Kody couldn't figure it out. She didn't get how to create air in a bubble where there wasn't any air pressure to begin with. She explained this to Briony, who shook her head.

"You're thinking too much. It's not about rationalizing how it works, it's about envisioning the outcome and making it happen."

Tristan spoke up and Kody shook her head at his inability to let any chance to disagree with Briony pass. "I've spent a lot of time with mages. Usually, there are words and objects they use. It's complex, not just thinking and doing."

Briony let out a huff. "Hu magic is overly complicated. They don't trust the ruakh so they need all the rules to make sure it does exactly what they want." She looked at Kody. "You need to trust the ruakh, and yourself. Trust your magic to know it's capable of what you're doing."

Kody frowned. "So, is it like you fill the bubble with air first? Or like you are blowing up a balloon?"

"Stop thinking!" Briony shoved Tristan toward Kody. "Here, try attacking her again, maybe grab her waist like you did this morning."

Kody gaped at her sister, the evil witch. Did she think that shoving her man crush at her would make her stop thinking? Good thing Tristan wouldn't go along with it . . .

Tristan just shrugged and stepped toward her.

Kody shrieked and tried to dart away, but Tristan caught her elbow with that blacksmith grip of his and pulled her into him. He held one arm in the air and used the other to force her against his chest.

Her mind jumped to a million places, not one about breaking his grip. She took a deep breath and closed her eyes. He smelled like peppermint and wood smoke. She squeezed her eyes tighter, trying to block out the intrusive thoughts. How was she supposed to push Tristan away with a burst of air when she didn't particularly want to shove him away? But he was only holding her for this demonstration, not because he wanted to. There. That was the thought that gave her the will to think of the magic. How could she want to stay in his arms when it meant something different to her than it did to him?

Kody thought of Briony's instructions. She dismissed thoughts of a bubble and instead found the place between her and Tristan. That part was easy, as every fiber of her being was well aware of every place they touched. Kody focused on those points. She wanted to be separate, for space to be between them, and so she would make it so. She imagined space between them, and then willed it to be all at once.

The force flung them apart. Kody landed on a cushion of air, her sister's eyes and swirls glowing as she carefully lowered her to the ground.

Tristan landed in the river.

Briony helped Kody to her feet. "That was excellent. Next time picture yourself like a tree, anchored to the eres, so you don't go flying too."

Kody rushed to the river where Tristan kicked against the current, fighting his way back to their small beach. Apparently, the river wasn't so lazy under the surface.

"Can you help him?" Kody asked her sister.

"No need. He's fine," Briony said, gesturing upriver.

Something large dragged against the surface of the water, moving fast toward Tristan, and then sunk under until it was out of sight.

"Is it going to eat him?" Kody asked, gripping her sister's arm.

"Please, do you really think I'd kill off your boyfriend?" Briony asked.

"He's not my—" Kody started but trailed off as Tristan rose weirdly out of the water until he was fully above the surface. He seemed to panic for a moment, then held on tight as the thing moved toward the bank.

Kody took a big step back as an enormous frog crawled out of the water, with Tristan clinging to something along its back. The frog was covered in a rainbow of neon colors, like a middle school girl's binder, which was weird. Tristan jumped off the frog as soon as it was on solid ground and, keeping his eyes on the creature, took several steps back until he was standing beside Kody.

"That was weird," Tristan said.

Kody just nodded and watched her sister approach the frog. "Thank you for coming, pretty girl," Briony said, stroking gently down the top of the frog's head Two more large, brightly colored frogs crawled out of the river behind the first.

"To be clear, why did you call the frogs?" Kody asked.

Briony turned and smiled at her companions. "So they can take us the rest of the way to Hivagora."

"I was afraid you were going to say that," Kody groaned.

"Trust me. By foot, the journey would take a week. With the help of our friends, we will be home in time for dinner."

"And how are we supposed to hang on to slimy frogs?" Kody asked.

"Please, they aren't slimy, and they have harnesses."

Tristan nodded. "Can confirm. They do have harnesses."

Kody shot Tristan a glance. "You're seriously okay with the frog travel?"

Tristan shrugged. "Sounds faster than a horse."

Kody turned and paced a few feet away, wiping her face with both hands.

Briony approached her and put a hand on her shoulder. "If you're really not comfortable, we can walk."

"No, I'm fine. I just needed a moment to get used to the idea." Kody let out a sharp breath. "Can I ride the purple and blue one?"

Briony laughed. They grabbed their packs, which Briony made magically waterproof, and took some time familiarizing themselves with the buckles and straps of the harnesses "in case they needed to get loosened quickly." Briony's words didn't exactly reassure Kody, but Tristan still strapped himself to a frog, so she couldn't exactly complain. He didn't even need to be making this trip except for her guilt-tripping him into coming.

Kody made her way up high on the frog's wet and slick, but not slimy, back. Her head was level with the frog's eyes—where, Briony explained, their heads would stay above water so they could breathe.

It took a few tries for Kody to find the right height, not so high as having most of her weight pushing down the frog's head, but also not so low as she would drown. The slope of the frog's back made an oddly perfect bed for Kody to lie on, her arms comfortably hanging onto the harness at chest level. If Kody lay her head to the left or right, she could almost imagine she was on a unique pool floaty getting ready for a nap in the sun. The water was cool and refreshing after the hot walk through the forest and, as she quickly adapted to the temperature change, Kody thought the swim upstream might not be so bad. If only she wasn't fully clothed, boots and all. Briony said their packs would be fine, but Kody wasn't looking forward to showing up to her ancestral home sopping wet.

The frog stretched out its limbs as if waking up from a nap, and then Kody launched forward. It took her a moment to realize the frog was still under her as they rocketed through the water in quick, jilting thrusts.

A howl exploded from Kody's right and she turned her head to see Briony sitting up, a fist in the air.

"What do you think of your first anura ride, sister?" Briony yelled loud enough to be heard over the crashing wake.

Kody laughed, at a loss for words, and glanced behind her to where Tristan's frog brought up the rear. He was wincing against the mist of water Kody's frog was kicking up, but she also saw that slight grin on his face as they reached incredible speeds.

The scenery around them shifted often from dense jungle-like forest to clearings and small beaches. Kody saw a family of giant frogs sunning on a fallen tree, and later she saw something that might have been an odd-colored bear.

The trees grew bigger and closer together the further up the river they went; their branches arching over the water, creating a dense canopy that stretched higher and higher yet always blocking out the direct sunlight. The canopy acted like a filter, casting a cool glow to the river below. Kody thought she could almost see better in this natural shade, spotting animals and interesting plants where before she'd only seen shadows.

"We're almost there!" Briony waved and pointed up toward a thick patch of foliage. Kody looked closer and noticed two people, a woman and a man in uniform, waving back.

The trees grew thicker along the river, growing over and intertwining with their partners on the opposite bank until the frogs entered a sort of tunnel. They passed several sets of open gates until the tunnel ended and they emerged on a shallow bank, while the river curved off to their right.

Two men and a woman, all in uniforms of green and brown, waited on the bank. As soon as Briony's frog bottomed out, not even out of the water, she slipped off her buckles and launched herself into the arms of one of the waiting men who caught her, lifting her off her feet. Kody's frog hit the bank and climbed from the water. The waiting woman assisted Kody with her buckles and helped her stand.

"Thank you," Kody said, her legs stiff under her.

"It's my pleasure, Your Highness," the woman said, bowing.

Kody didn't know how to respond but was saved from the embarrassment as Briony grabbed her arm and pulled her toward the man she'd been embracing.

"Kody, I would like to introduce you to Havu, my love," Briony said.

"Your Highness," Havu said, bowing, the front of his uniform sopping wet from Briony's hug.

He took Kody slightly off guard with his long, flowing platinum blond hair and pale alabaster skin that showed in stark contrast to the green swirls covering his arms, neck, and face. Kody was at once thankful for her darker tone. She never would have been able to hide her green swirls on Earth if she were as light as him.

"It's good to meet you," Kody said, and turned as Tristan reached her side.

Havu frowned at Tristan. "And who is this?"

"This is my friend, Tristan, who kindly agreed to travel with us," Kody said, stepping in before anyone tried to make Tristan feel unwelcomed.

"He's another of the Misplaced," Briony said.

“Ah, I see. It is a pleasure,” Havu said, nodding. Tristan nodded back.

“Right. Shall we head home?” Briony said, gesturing toward a short set of stairs leading from the beach.

The man who’d helped Tristan from his frog approached them. "If I may?”

“Oh, of course,” Briony said, and Kody glanced at her, confused. The man’s swirls glowed across his arms and face, and a strong wind took up around Kody and the others, as if she stood over a grate. It lasted only a moment, and as her clothes fell back into place, she found herself perfectly dry.

Kody reached up to feel her hair, worried it would be all over the place, but the neat triple row of French braids felt perfect. She turned to her sister. “Is this why you offered to braid my hair this morning?” She’d thought the offer a little random, but she’d never had a sister to braid her hair before, so she’d accepted.

Briony grinned. “Of course.”

Kody smiled and shook her head as Briony and Havu led the way off the beach. She checked for Tristan, but he was at her side.

“Are you getting strong Legolas vibes?” he asked, gesturing toward Havu.

Kody covered a snort and punched Tristan in the shoulder.

He grinned, and they ascended the stairs to a hard-packed dirt path that led into what could only be described as a magical Elv forest city.

Chapter Twelve

The city teamed with life, more life than Kody had ever seen in one place. Plants grew over, around, and under everything, and birds and pollinating insects of every color flew from branch to bud to leaf and back. Duck mothers led their ducklings along the road and bunnies munched clover in front of and on top of shops and houses.

And then there were the people. Hundreds of people, of every shape and size, wearing dresses and robes and pants and tunics, all made of flowing gauzy fabric in lovely natural and earth tones. The people came in every shade common among humans back on Earth but in a variety she had rarely seen in real life. And every single one of them had bright green swirls all over their exposed flesh and pointed ears sticking out of every texture and color of hair imaginable. Now and then she saw a person with no swirls and couldn't help but examine them closely, to see what about them led them to a life among the Elv.

As they passed a steady flow of people, many of them paid no attention to Kody or her party, but every now and again, someone would notice Briony and nod respectfully or share a handshake or hug with her before allowing her to move on. The few that greeted her the most familiarly would shoot a look over Briony's shoulder at Kody with knowing interest.

The people flowed along the road, in and out of shops and houses and structures of every kind. There were buildings built into the ground and covered with moss, others sat like tree houses on thick branches overhead, some seemed to grow intertwined with nearby trees, and others, still, built of stone with architecture similar to the castle in Rohap.

Kody silently wished she wouldn't end up in a treehouse for the night. She'd never been known for sleepwalking, but there was a first time for everything.

Rope and wood bridges stretched between trees high above and Kody caught Tristan's eye as they watched a small toddler running across a rope bridge to a waiting parent.

Tristan grinned at her unease. "Afraid of heights?"

"No, you?" Kody asked.

"Not yet."

Briony led Kody deeper into the forest, where the trees grew thicker and thicker around until she was certain someone could carve a full house into their trunk. In fact, she thought she spied a few doors hinting at such dwellings.

Their path wound through a lovely garden, blooming with more flower varieties than Kody knew existed, and led to a wide set of stairs grown from the roots of a giant tree, larger than any other in the forest. The trunk stretched high into the sky, disappearing in the surrounding canopy. Vines of flowering wisteria climbed and twisted up the bark, framing windows and small terraces along the way. Root stairs led up to two ornately carved doors.

Before Kody could get a good look at what the carvings depicted, the doors were flung wide by two Elv in uniforms similar to Havu's. Elvs in flowing earth-toned clothing poured out of the tree in a mass that revolved around a man in loose-fitting moss-green pants, a flowing brown shirt, and a spring-green robe billowing around him.

A woman with a clipboard keeping pace with the group pushed her way through to the center. "But Your Majesty, the northern city is demanding an answer today," the woman said.

"Later, later," the man in the middle of the chaos said while making shooing gestures. "Is she here yet?" he asked, as his eyes roamed the surrounding steps.

Kody watched as his eyes landed first on Briony, and his face lit into a smile. And then their eyes connected. Her father took several quick steps down the stairs until he stood just a step above Kody and slowed. His face was wider and rounder than hers, similar to Briony, but he had those familiar eyes and the same nose Kody saw every day in the mirror. His skin was mahogany swirled with emerald, and his eyes were wrapped in laugh lines.

He reached out a hand and Kody took it. He held her hand in his for one long moment and pulled her into a hug. She sunk into the embrace, her heart and spirit melting. The next thing she knew, a warm presence smashed against her back and Kody smelled the familiar scent of her sister sandwiching her into the hug.

When at last they broke the embrace, Kody's chest was full and her sister grinned before patting Kody's head.

"Dad, this is Kody," Briony introduced.

Kody found his red-rimmed eyes tracking along her features as if he couldn't get enough of the sight of her. He held her hand again between his own and brought it to his face, kissing the back of her hand.

"Kody," Callum said, as if feeling out the pronunciation. "I have waited far, far too long to see you returned to me, my daughter. You were lost, but never forgotten." He kissed her hand again as tears ran down his face.

Kody swallowed hard at the words, trying not to lose it.

Briony stepped forward again and wiped his face with her

palm. "No need to cry any longer, Dad. We have her back and she's wonderful."

Kody chuckled, trying to break the swarm of emotions that attempted to consume her. "Besides, you don't even know me yet. I might chew with my mouth open and then you'll wanna give me back."

"True," Briony agreed with a deadpan expression. "Too bad we're stuck with you, since the spell's broken permanently."

"We can always chuck her in the river," Callum said in an absolutely serious voice, his brown eyes sparkling.

Kody burst out laughing, both shocked and relieved at the break from emotion. She was delighted to have come all this way and found her long-lost father was perfectly sarcastic.

Briony slapped her on the back. "See? I said you'd love it here."

"And who is this extra you've brought to us, my daughter?" Callum asked, turning toward Tristan.

Kody wasn't sure who he was taking to, but thankfully, Briony answered. "That's another of the Misplaced. His name is Tristan. Kody found him not long after arriving and he helped her transition."

Tristan stepped up to stand just a level below Kody.

The king nodded to Tristan. "Thank you for helping my daughter. You are welcome in the city for as long as you wish to stay."

"Thank you," Tristan replied with a small bow.

A small spark of anxiety stirred in Kody's chest. She hoped Tristan stayed for a while. She wasn't ready to see him go.

Havu exited the tree doorway and bowed to the king. "The Princess and her guest's rooms are ready, Your Majesty."

Kody blinked. She hadn't seen Havu leave, and come to think of it, they now stood just the five of them on the root steps, completely alone as the crowd of advisers and people in uniform had also melted away while she embraced her father.

"Shall I let you settle in before dinner, then?" Callum asked, offering his arm to Kody.

She smiled and took his arm, and he led her up the last few steps. When they were on even footing, Kody was surprised to realize he was only a few inches taller than her. His presence, commanding yet gentle, made her feel safe.

He led her into a tree that transformed into a grand atrium with rooms and passages spanning in every direction. On each side were two identical grand staircases that looked grown out of the tree and spiraled higher than Kody could see, wrapping around the hollow inside.

"You may ask for anything you need, and it will be brought. I will leave you to your sister to show to your rooms," Callum said, patting Kody's arm. "I shall see you soon for dinner." He bowed his head to Kody, who sort of bowed back awkwardly as he smiled and disappeared through a doorway. Kody saw someone in uniform appear at his side a moment later, and her father's shoulders seemed to droop.

"Are you ready to get cleaned up?" Briony asked, and Kody nearly jumped, pulled suddenly out of the trance that was her father's presence. When he spoke to her, it was like she was the only one in the room, and she felt a little lonely with him gone. "You get used to it," Briony said with a sad smile. "Come on."

Briony grabbed her arm and pulled her up the staircase to the left.

Kody looked back to find Tristan.

"Come, we take the other staircase," Havu told Tristan with a frown as he tried to follow Kody.

"Are you okay, Tristan?" Kody asked, not wanting to abandon him, and feeling a little weird parting ways.

"Yeah, I'll be fine," he said shortly, before following Havu.

Kody sighed as he crossed the atrium, but Briony pulled her up the stairs.

"We aren't climbing all the way up, are we?"

Briony laughed. "God no."

They climbed the distance of about two floors before Briony

tugged Kody through an open doorway that led to a long pathway. Kody couldn't help but suspect the path was only a giant branch with vines growing up on either side to serve as guard rails.

"Don't worry about your Tristan," Briony said, stepping out onto what appeared to be a solid path. "He's in the guest wing. Your rooms are with ours in the royal family apartments."

Kody followed her sister carefully, stepping lightly. "It just seems like maybe Havu doesn't like him very much." Halfway across the branch, Kody was sure she felt it swaying, but Briony didn't seem to notice.

"He's just like that. You know how some men are all frowns in situations where they aren't comfortable? Havu's second in command of security, so he's distrusting of everyone and rarely comfortable enough to relax."

"That makes sense."

"Trust me, once you get to know him, you'll see he's a completely different person."

They reached a spot where the branch forked and in the center of the intersection was a large basket with a flat bottom hanging from ropes stretching far above. The basket resembled something Kody would expect to see hanging from a hot-air balloon, and a bad feeling crept in.

"This isn't what I think it is, is it?" Kody asked.

Briony rolled her eyes. "You said you didn't want to walk the stairs, didn't you?" She found a latch on the side of the basket and opened a panel so Kody could step inside. Kody did so, *carefully*.

"This lift only leads to the royal apartments, and only a member of the royal family can run it." She followed Kody in, causing the basked to rock a little, and closed the door. "Here, place your hand on the round part there."

Kody placed her hand on the round knob of wood, and the basket shot into the air.

"See! Even the lift knows you're family!" Briony laughed as Kody gripped the side of the basket, her knuckles turning white.

"How does it run?" Kody asked, swallowing a scream as she tried to keep her voice level.

"Magic," Briony said gleefully, the wind blowing their clothes in every direction.

Kody would have rolled her eyes if she wasn't so busy trying to keep them in her head. They rose higher and higher until the pathways and structures below looked like a figure set, and finally, the basket slowed to a stop. Briony stepped out onto a new giant branch while Kody stood frozen, still gripping the basket as hard as she could. She unclenched one hand, then the other. She tested her feet to make sure they could move.

"I didn't know you were afraid of heights," Briony said with a small, apologetic smile.

"I'm not." Kody stepped out onto the branch path beside Briony. "I just like knowing how something works before it shoots me in the air."

Briony snorted and led the way.

Her room wasn't on the ground level, but it was open and airy in all the right ways, while still feeling super stable. The flooring was wood paneling, and a lovely cream wallpaper with small, intricately painted leaves spread from wall to wall. There was a sitting room with a desk and bookshelf and a few couches, a bedroom with a large four-poster bed and a quilt made of beautiful earth tones. Flowing light clothes that were already in her size filled the closet, and the bathroom was a whole experience. A waterfall flowed out of a stone wall, the water crossing the room as a small river and filling a deep pool on the far end. The room opened to a spectacular view of trees and flowering vines through a small transparent cloth, the only protection from the elements.

"Don't worry, it's spelled to shield from the outside. It's quite private," Briony reassured her.

The space was perfect. Kody sunk down on the plush bed and ran her hand over the quilt. It was soft in that way only an old, well-loved quilt could be. As she examined it, her eyes found intricate shapes stitched into the complex pattern.

"That's one your mother made," Briony said, sitting on the nightstand by the bed. Kody glanced up at her, not ready to believe it, and her sister nodded. "Dad still uses one just like it, but with different patterns. She loved quilting."

Kody pet the blanket gently, too stunned to speak at having not just a family, but even a family heirloom.

Briony stood. "Well, you should wash up and change. Take a soak or enjoy the waterfall. I'll come get you for dinner. If you need anything, I'm just a level above you, okay?"

Kody nodded, and Briony snuck in for one more hug. "Welcome home," she whispered before leaving Kody's new rooms.

Kody sat for a long time, soaking in the space and everything she'd seen and learned. After a time, she wiped her eyes on her sleeves and did, in fact, enjoy a nice soak in the warm pool before rinsing off in the waterfall, washing and styling her hair with the products she found.

The water was refreshing, but she felt off balance. How could she keep a level head and make a rational decision about her future when her heart was so full of hope and joy? She wanted to dismiss her need for a plan and live in the moment. Enjoy this city for what it was and get to know her family, but a part of her tensed at the thought, as if bracing for a punch in the stomach. Everything seemed perfect with Briony and her father, but everything had also seemed perfect with countless foster families who'd taken her in over the years, and she knew DNA didn't make a difference. How many other kids in the system had blood relatives who dropped them at the first inconvenience?

She needed to stay focused and learn about these people and their world so she could decide if she wanted to stay, or go back to Rohap and strike up a different sort of life.

She wasn't sure what to wear to dinner but decided on some loose pants and a flowing mustard-yellow top. Briony would tell her if she needed to change. After a life in dark colors, Kody found she enjoyed yellow and green and the other earth tones and pastels the Elv commonly wore.

Not sure what else to do, Kody exited her rooms onto the long branch path and found the stairs Briony had pointed out. On the next level was a similar apartment to Kody's, built into the side of the tree, but with a darker stain on the door. Kody knocked, and a small green spark lit the doorknob. The door swung open and Kody ducked her head in.

"Come in," Briony called.

Kody entered the sitting room, similar to her own, but lived in. The bookcases were full, and the couches covered in pillows and throw blankets. The coffee table had a mug resting next to a book, and the desk was covered in papers. Living green vines covered the wallpaper and a warm rust-colored rug cushioned the floor. Briony popped her head out of a side room, her hands busy pinning her hair.

"Good, I forgot to tell you dinner is super casual." Briony wore an outfit similar to Kody's, but in browns and greens. She gestured for Kody to follow her into the bedroom. The room would have been a close copy to Kody's if it wasn't for the large tree growing out of her bedroom floor, the floorboards pulled up around it to make space. The tree was odd, with chalky white bark and lovely blue star-shaped leaves.

Kody eyed the tree wearily and sat on the bed. "Why do you have a tree in your room?"

"It's an Elv custom." Briony stuck another pin in her hair to hold a curl in place, then joined Kody on the bed. "It's tradition for Elv to show interest in another by planting something in their garden. A symbol of their budding love. Over the centuries it became a little more interesting, and now it has a lot more to do with breaking and entering and vandalism than just gardening."

"So, Havu planted this?" Kody asked, not really picturing the frowning platinum blond Elv doing something so mundane as ripping up floorboards.

"He did. I've had a few suitors over the years, and let me tell you, it's always a pain to clean up when someone you aren't interested in plants a bush in your living room, not to mention the sometimes political implications of ripping it out and chucking it off the tree."

"What was different about Havu?" Kody asked, still trying to understand her sister's boyfriend. He seemed distant and rigid in a way Tristan never had been.

"You know, I don't think I ever paid him much attention at first. Our family always ruled here in Hivagora, but there were other Elv royal lines in cities across the Twoshy. When the Hu invaded, some were wiped out, others displaced. Havu comes from one of those old lines. In another life where the Hu hadn't invaded, he would be in line to be king of some Elv castle." Briony rolled her eyes. "And he's obsessed with it. The castle doesn't even stand anymore, but he still thinks about where he'd be. Anyway, when the tree popped up, I wasn't even sure who did it until I saw him leaning against the railing outside, twirling a blue leaf a few days later." Briony smiled as if remembering. "Even the tree he picked was a joke."

"What do you mean?"

Briony gestured to the tree. "It's called a cheer tree. It has medicinal uses, but just focus on the name. Would you ever associate something with the name cheer in it with Havu?"

Kody giggled. She would not.

"Exactly! I didn't believe it was him at first, and I think that's how he got me. I was interested. I wanted to know why he picked that plant, and before you know it, I realized there was so much more to him, and I fell."

"So you didn't rip up his tree."

"Nope. Instead, I ripped out a rose bush I'd been saving from a really handsome Elv. Remind me to point him out to you. I wasn't that into him, but Havu got really jealous when he saw it, so I was keeping it around for leverage."

Kody laughed. "How did he get up here if the lift doesn't work for him?"

"There are other ways up here, just none so direct or private. Everything else would put a visitor behind a checkpoint before reaching our rooms."

Kody nodded. "Is it a gender thing? The men are always the ones to do the planting?"

"Of course not. It's just whoever catches feelings first and wants the other to know. Why? Thinking of planting something in Tristan's bedroom?" Briony smiled and dug her elbow into Kody's ribs.

Kody laughed and pushed her away. "No, I was just curious. Tristan wouldn't get it even if I did."

"But you do like him." It wasn't quite a question.

"Well, yeah, but I just got out of a bad relationship. I think it's too soon to jump into another."

Briony's eyes got big. "Really? Okay, now you have to tell the whole story."

And so Kody did. She told Briony about Roger, and the way he'd locked her out of her own home, and how everything she owned was trapped inside. And then Kody realized something.

Absolutely none of that mattered anymore.

She'd left that entire world behind with no way to return. It didn't matter that she didn't have her social security card, or her college diploma, or even the scrapbook of memories she kept of every foster home growing up. The only piece of Earth Kody still had was her necklace, a bridge for her to her past.

It didn't really matter, but it did. She had nothing from her past. Her rooms were lovely, but they weren't hers. Briony's rooms were filled with little pieces of her life spread about. Kody's was filled with pieces someone else had picked out.

She felt like a visitor in the forest. Like this was just another temporary home, one she would leave at an unforeseen date, no matter how much she wanted to stay or it felt like home. But it didn't matter. She fingered the smooth silver at her neck and took a deep breath. If she chose to stay, it wouldn't be for anyone but herself, and she would build a new life.

Chapter Thirteen

The family dining room and general family meeting place was an ornate garden, suspended in the treetops. It looked like the forest floor but swayed ever so slightly—adding to the disorientation. When Kody stepped into the garden, she was tackled by a figure in pale lavender.

"Oh, my dear! Returned at last," the woman whispered into Kody's neck while hugging her tight. Kody tensed at first but relaxed into the hug when it didn't seem to go anywhere. After a long moment, the woman released Kody and held her at arm's length. "Let me get a good look at you. Your mother, Isleen, was a dear friend of mine. We grew up together and I can see her in your face."

Minda, queen of the Elv and Kody's stepmother, slowly stroked Kody's cheek while she spoke. Kody didn't know what to say. She'd been nervous to meet this woman, worrying some old family dynamic might make the queen resent Kody, but she'd been wrong. Minda was lovely. She was shorter than Kody and petite, like Briony, but there was steel in her grip. Her cool brown complexion and collection of tight, elegant curls draped around her face to frame her perfectly pouty lips, exactly like Briony's.

"Thanks, Mom, missed you too," Briony drawled at Kody's side.

Kody's stepmother rolled her eyes and pulled her daughter into a hug with a sigh. "Yes, my daughter, I missed you so much in the five days you were gone," she said in a bored voice before pulling away, grinning, and pinching her daughter's cheek. "You got some sun on your trip."

Briony batted away her mom's affection. "That happens when you're not cooped up in the forest all year."

Kody glanced reflexively at the tree canopy above, filtering the light and casting a gentle glow on everything below.

"Come, let's eat." Minda took Kody's arm in hers and gently led her down a tree-covered path. "The menfolk beat you here and will eat all the food. I like your Tristan, by the way. He's a sweet boy."

"What?" Briony exclaimed, stopping in her tracks. "You've spoken to him for all of a few minutes and you already approve of mister broody? It's been ten years and you still make Havu jump through hoops for your approval."

"Calm down, dear," Minda said, taking Briony's arm and patting it gently. "Tristan is much easier to read than Havu."

"Whatever, just admit you have a favorite daughter and be done with it."

Minda winked at Kody before addressing Briony. "Keep pestering me about Havu and I might pick a favorite."

The path led them around a stand of trees and over a pond before leading to an old weeping willow, its thick leafy branches stretching to the ground. Briony stepped in front of them and pulled back a section of branches. Minda gestured for Kody to go first, and she ducked under the leaves.

The first thing Kody noticed under the willow tree were the lights. Hundreds of tiny globes floated under the branches, lighting the space with faintly green light. The space under the tree was large, easily fitting a round table and chairs on one side of the trunk, with lounge chairs and plush couches grouped together on the other end. Tristan, Havu, and Callum sat waiting for them.

"Ah, there they are," Callum called at Kody's appearance. "Come, have a seat."

Kody took a chair between her father and Tristan while Briony sat across from her between her mother and Havu.

Dinner was casual and relaxed. Kody and Tristan talked about life on Earth, while Callum and Minda told of life in Hivagora, and of Kody's first few years. Briony talked about fun things to do around the city, making plans in the next few days to show her and Tristan everything, and Havu sat quietly and observed, his expression blank and unreadable.

Servers ducked through the branches to refill glasses, replace trays, and transition dinner to dessert. Kody filled herself with cookies dipped in creamy chocolate mousse, and eventually they all settled onto the nearby couches, full and sedated. A servant parted the willow branches, letting in a small breeze, and they sat as the evening grew dark and watched the fireflies, or some similar magical variety, as they danced over the garden.

When they said their goodnights, Callum pulled Kody into another tight embrace. "I take a break in the late morning for a walk in between meetings. If your sister doesn't monopolize all of your time, come join me."

Kody nodded. "I'd like that."

"Perfect."

They said goodnight and Tristan found her side as they left the garden.

"What do you think?" he asked her low enough not to be overheard.

Kody thought about it for a moment, and shook her head. "It all seems too good to be true."

Tristan smiled and nodded once. "It's a lot to take in, but try not to miss the moments that matter. Not everyone gets their happily ever after."

They reached Kody's apartment and Briony moved in to give

her a hug goodnight while Havu escorted Tristan back to the lower levels, where they both had rooms.

Kody lay in bed worrying about bugs flying into her breezy open bedroom and hovering around her face as she slept, but she found none. It was then she also realized how cool the city of Hivagora was. Since the moment Kody had fallen into the Twoshy, she'd been hot and sweaty. In Tristan's apartment, at night, and even on their journey through the forest, Kody had continually had a small sheen of sweat on the back of her neck and in other various places. She tried to think when the weather had changed to the moderate temperature it was now. Swimming upstream via frog, she'd been soaked from the journey, and when the waiting attendant had dried her, she hadn't realized the temperature was for once comfortable.

Kody relaxed into her pillow, smelling lightly of lavender, and sighed with contentment. In the heat of a scorching summer, this city was comfortable and cool. As long as the temperature didn't drop to freezing in the winter, she thought she might very well enjoy living in this magical forest.

Kody awoke the next morning feeling fantastic. It was the first morning in a long time she didn't wake in a puddle of sweat. A light breeze blew through her room, and small birds chirped outside her window. She pulled on a flowy robe and wandered into her sitting room, wishing she had a phone to call Briony, to see when breakfast was or when and where she needed to be.

A small table sat just inside her front door, covered with food and a teapot. Kody smiled. Being served was something she could easily get used to. The tea was warm and spiced with something lovely, and her accompanying eggs and fruit turnover were wonderful. After eating, she took a shower in her waterfall and got dressed for the day.

With nothing left to do, Kody exited her rooms, stepping out onto the long path and the open air. She leaned against the railing and looked down. Her stomach didn't exactly turn, but she regretted that fourth turnover. She stepped back from the railing and took a deep breath. She had a hard time understanding how high up she really was, and she thought perhaps she should never think about it again.

"Elv don't fly," Briony said from behind Kody, causing her to jump. "Whoa now, don't test the theory." Briony took her arm and pulled her a little further from the railing.

"Has anyone ever fallen?"

Briony laughed. "No, there's a railing."

"What about small children climbing it?"

Briony gave her a weird look. "Children aren't that stupid. Are Hu children that stupid? How do they make it to maturity? Never mind. Come, I have much of the city to show you and we're losing daylight."

Kody laughed as Briony grabbed her arm and pulled her to the basket lift. The ride down caused Kody's stomach to fly out of the basket at some point, and her legs felt a little shaky descending the staircase into the atrium tree.

Briony dragged Kody first to a row of workshops, Elvs sewing and stitching, working metal and wood. Briony introduced her to all of them by name, and the Elvs greeted her, welcoming her home. When they left the last clothes dyer, Briony whisked her off to a market with shops selling anything Kody could ever need. Briony introduced her to shoppers and shopkeepers, every face and name bleeding into one as she tried to find things that stood out about each. Olivia was the tall willowy Elv who sold wooden spoons, and Marc was the short round Elv with piercings lining his pointed ears who sold decorative pillows. Kinf, a man buying socks, was very friendly and didn't want to let go of her hand after she offered it to shake, forgetting the Elv didn't do that.

"Should we find Tristan?" Kody asked as they left a shoe shop, and a handsome Elv with a nose ring stopped them to introduce himself.

"You're meeting Dad, right?" Briony asked, pushing the tall

nose ring guy back on the path after he'd held Kody's hand and wished her the most wonderful reunion with her people.

"Yes. He said late morning. I don't even know what time it is."

"Oh, yes, it's tricky without the sun. Remind me to teach you that spell. How about when you go to get Dad I'll find Tristan and we will meet up with you for lunch?"

"That sounds great," Kody replied over the shoulder of a new man with red hair who went out of his way to introduce himself.

Now and then they passed an Elv who didn't seem interested in meeting Kody, and a few who nearly seemed offended at the sight of her. When they encountered these people, Briony laughed it off and led Kody to see something new and exciting.

Kody wasn't sure if Briony was getting bored or if she sensed her sister's annoyance, but next she took her to the library. It was a beautiful old building built out of the stump of a fallen giant tree and wound down into the ground. The librarian was a shy girl with purple hair that Kody thought might make a great friend as she shared novel recommendations. If only Kody could find a way to power on her phone, maybe she could copy out books from her reading app and translate them. Copyright be damned.

After the library, Briony led Kody back to the largest tree in the center of the city. They were stopped by countless good-natured Elv trying to introduce themselves to Kody. When at last they reached the tree, Briony showed Kody the paths to take to reach their father's office. When they entered, Callum dismissed his attendants along with their questions and clipboards and greeted his daughters.

Briony told Kody she'd retrieve her for lunch and left the newly reunited father and daughter for their morning walk. Callum led Kody through a back door of his office that opened to an overgrown wooded path.

Chapter Fourteen

Every part of the city Kody had seen so far was a neatly manicured picture-perfect portrait of nature, but the path her father led her down felt like a magical forest where any plant might transform into a nymph and speak to her. The path was dotted with the occasional leaf, and plant life grew and blended in a wildly unkempt mess that somehow made the outdoor space feel even more alive.

They walked for a time, Callum content with the silence, but a question ate away at Kody.

"May I ask you what my birth name is?" she said at last.

He didn't respond immediately, continuing his slow wandering pace down the path, and Kody followed at his side, hoping her question hadn't somehow been impolite. She didn't want to offend this man before she'd had a chance to know him. After a long moment, they came to a small pool of water, crystal clear and shaded by an old, gnarled tree, its roots dipping down into the pool.

"Names hold much meaning for our people," he said at last. "A person's name rarely follows them through life, but may grow and change along with the soul it describes. Your sister, for example, was not born Briony."

Her father knelt beside the pool and slipped his hand in, causing a ripple that distorted the view of the many colorful stones at the bottom of the water. He cupped one hand and brought it to his mouth to drink, then shook the excess back into the pool. Where each drop landed, a ripple pulsed out, and a moment later Kody spotted what she had believed to be just another jewel toned rock move up and inspect the impact point of a water drop. The small fish, a beautiful golden yellow, found nothing on the surface and slowly swam closer to where Kody and her father stood.

She met her father's eyes, and he grinned at her before shrugging and reaching into the flowy over robe he wore. He rummaged around for a moment and pulled out a fist. He held it out to Kody.

Kody hesitated, remembering a boy making the same gesture when she was young, but he'd dropped something slimy in her hand, and she'd never been so trusting again. But this was her father, and if he was the sort to carry slimy things in his pockets, it would be good to know now.

She held out her hand, and he dropped a handful of small seeds into her waiting palm. They were tiny and roundish, and she had absolutely no idea what they were. Her father picked out one small seed and threw it into the water. Kody watched and nearly dropped them all in shock as dozens of jewel covered fish rose from the bottom of the pool and swarmed the seed.

Callum laughed. It was a deep belly laugh and caught Kody off guard. She smiled, watching as his laugh shrank to a chuckle, and he placed a hand on her shoulder. "They are lovely, are they not? Keep feeding them or they may grow legs and come for us."

Kody hoped the small smile lingering on her father's lips meant it was a joke, but at this point, she would believe anything was possible in this strange world. She pinched a few seeds and threw them into the water, and marveled at the rainbow of colors flashing through the water as the fish swarmed their offering.

"I hope you have more in those pockets. I doubt this will tide them over," Kody said as she threw another pinch of seed into the pond.

Her father, to her relief, pulled out another handful, and joined her in feeding the desperate fish.

"Do not worry about feeding them all. My dears are fat and well fed. This seed is not nutritious, but they go mad for it. My aquarist is forever telling me I spoil them, but I like sweet things that are bad for me. Why shouldn't these creatures, who bring me so much joy, receive the same?"

Kody sprinkled the last of her seed into the pool and watched her father as he watched the fish, an adorable little smile on his face while he rooted for different fish to get the treat first. She suddenly remembered this man was the king of all Elv, and wasn't sure how that thought, which had seemed so important before, had somehow slipped her mind.

When his seeds were gone, Callum led Kody to a bench made of woven branches on the water's edge where they could watch the fish float lazily in the pool, looking for missed treats before settling back on the bottom for an afternoon nap.

"When Briony was young, maybe four or five, she was always climbing trees, going higher and higher. It drove her mother mad, always worrying she would fall, which she did often enough. One day we were enjoying the autumn leaf fall, and your sister was climbing and climbing away, up an old oak. She wandered out onto a branch with none beneath her to catch onto in case she fell, so of course she lost her grip."

"Was she okay?"

Her father patted her shoulder. "Her mother used her magic and asked the tree to produce new growth and catch her. After the oak set her gently on the eres, and your sister endured a scolding, she immediately climbed back up and surpassed the spot where she fell."

Right, they had magic. Of course they didn't mind small children climbing to their deaths. Briony's comments about Elv children not being that stupid made Kody roll her eyes.

"Her mother tried to call her back, but she would not listen. I told her mother then, it was as if she were the briony, always climbing higher and higher to find the sun. That became her name, and as sometimes happens, this second name fit her in more ways than I could ever know. Much as the briony vine, your sister is always growing and always stretching, reaching for anything she can spot in the distance, never satisfied in existing only where she is planted."

Kody smiled. "From what I know of her, that seems to fit her well. She's someone I believe can accomplish anything she sets herself to."

Her father nodded. "When you were born, you were our Aylass, the moonlight through the canopy."

Aylass. That was her name.

Her whole life, she'd wondered what her true name was. Had anyone even named her or had she been so unwanted? Most foster and adopted had their birth name, but that was just one more place where Kody was set apart.

Aylass, she was Aylass, moonlight through the canopy . . . But she didn't feel like moonlight. She didn't feel like an Aylass. Aylass would be a lovely, elegant girl who glided through life wearing fine gowns like she was born for them. Kody frowned.

Her father nodded again. "You are no longer Aylass. That name was lost to you when you were taken from us, but the loss of a name is no loss at all, instead it is a symbol of change and growth. Kody is who you are now, and now is all that matters."

Something swelled in Kody's chest. It was exactly what she needed to hear, even if she hadn't known it. His words expressed acceptance of her exactly as she was.

"Tell me, what does Kody mean to you?" her father asked.

Kody thought for a moment but shook her head. "I don't know. I'm sure it has a meaning, but I don't remember ever looking it up.

The social worker who named me said I looked like a little bear, and Kody sounds a little like one of the bear names, so she picked it. Not really anything special."

Callum nodded knowingly. "Courage."

"What?"

"Bears represent courage to our people. There is also an old legend about bears having the courage to evolve and the ability to be open-minded. To grow in your other world, and then to come here and discover this one, I believe courage is exactly what you have. Kody, you are well-named, and I am honored by the person you have become."

His voice was a little thick, something shining in his eyes, and Kody looked away, focusing on a purple and chartreuse fish swimming near her feet. If she just focused on that one little fish, and the flash of colors it made in the water, the pressure behind her eyes would disappear and she wouldn't start crying.

Her father put his hand on her back, and the gesture broke something in her, and the tears fell. Undoing all the barriers and walls she'd built around her heart to keep it safe and unbroken. He pulled her close to his side, and they sat watching the fish and quietly crying over their lost time and new beginning.

Back in Callum's office, he explained the power structure of the Elv. He was king, and while Kody thought that would mean he was the most powerful Elv in the forest, she was surprised to learn he didn't have the gift to use magic. The Elv didn't need his power; they needed his wisdom, guidance, and leadership. He explained that the forest lent a bit of its power to the ruler, granting him or her a different type of power. One better suited for leading than for shaping ruakh, and he was content as he was. Kody wondered if that was what gave him such a presence.

Callum showed Kody maps of the forest detailing where other Elv settlements and cities lived. He explained many of the smaller towns were separatists. Elv, who believed their calling was to be one with nature and that their ancestors venturing out on the continent building stone and brick castles, was the ultimate cause of the fall of Elv kind. Hivagora, with its mesh of styles, was hated by some small parties of Elv, and Hu were seen as outsiders or enemies. Her father frowned as he spoke of the political problems and Kody couldn't help but remember the few Elv who'd shot her nasty looks during her tour with Briony.

"Most of our people only wished to live a prosperous life, protected in their forest where they know an enemy could never uproot them," Callum continued, running a thumb over the frown in her forehead. "Everyone who met your mother adored her, and once our people have a chance to know you, I believe the same will be said of your legacy. The politics are good to know as you move through the world but are nothing that should trouble you."

Before long, Briony arrived with Tristan in tow, and they said goodbye to Callum and ventured back out into the city. Men and women still stopped them to speak with Kody, which Tristan seemed to find endlessly annoying until a cute brunette Elv stopped him to chat and Briony pulled him the other way.

They had lunch in a little café on the edge of the river, watching ducks and otters float by with the occasional giant frog.

Briony ordered an extra meal and left Tristan and Kody to enjoy the river while she took lunch to an on-duty Havu.

Kody smiled and waved her sister off, promising they would wait for her. She turned back to Tristan, who was watching her oddly.

"What?" Self-consciousness straightened her posture.

"I'm glad you found your family," he said after a moment with a soft smile she hadn't seen before.

"Thank you." Kody grew quiet, not sure if she should ask what was on her mind. She took a sip of her carbonated fruit juice and asked anyway. "What happened to your family?"

"They died," he said with a shrug. "I was an only child, and they both came from small families, and here we are a century later. I have some distant cousins and met them once, but it was super awkward." He looked down. "I could tell they didn't want to be there. They didn't see me as anything other than a spectacle, just one more of the Misplaced, and my home country had a lot of Misplaced. So one day I asked the tavern owner who was hosting me if I could have a horse and I rode. I reached Leronia first, the Misplaced there is a nice girl, but the role of national freak was taken so I kept going and I reached Rohap, one of the few nations of the Twoshy that didn't have any young heirs to steal at the time the spell snatched us all. They weren't used to having Misplaced to deal with, so they were a little more accepting. Then I met Rawford who offered to teach me a trade. So every time I traveled, I found a horse and I made my way to Rohap."

"That must have been hard."

"I never really minded. It taught me a trade as a way to provide for myself and not rely on others."

Kody nodded. "I need to find one of those."

Tristan shrugged and looked out into the river. "I think you have time. You have a family now. Spend the time you need getting to know them and let an occupation just fall into place."

"You're probably right," Kody agreed. "If the positions were reversed, I would do anything for my family. I don't know why letting someone do it for me is so much harder." She knew it was true, but still that fear of being too much of a burden, and the anxiety over a lack of a plan didn't leave. As much as she'd tried to stay neutral, she couldn't help but feel the pull of family sway her planning. How could she ever go back to Rohap when her family was here and so excited to know her? The only pull to Rohap was Tristan, and that thought was an even bigger landmine. She wanted to be the independent, level-headed woman she saw in her mind, but too many emotional connections threatened to undo her.

Briony returned a short time later, and they spent the afternoon roaming the city. They toured the forges, which Kody found a little boring, but Tristan made friends with a grizzled old woman, a blacksmith with a hunched back and wiry muscles. Kody wondered how old the Elv must be for her age to show so deeply, but Briony only shook her head. "She's probably older than the Twoshy."

The tour of the water reservoirs and aqueducts at the very top of the forest canopy was an experience. They took three hanging baskets to reach a staggering height just below the leaf level. From there they were carefully escorted past layers and layers of football-field-sized leaves, the temperature growing steadily as they rose, until at last they stepped into the sun. The great green expanse of the treetops radiated heat. Kody broke out in a sweat and mentally begged their guide to take them back below the leaves.

They walked along the spines of giant leaves, the edges of each blade turned up to collect and store rainwater in massive reservoirs. Heated by the sun, this topmost level supplied the hot water through the city, this magical tree staying evergreen through the winter while others died around it.

When at last the sun became unbearable, the guide took them below a few layers of leaves to the cooler water reservoirs, shaded gently from the sun, but still brighter and hotter than the city below. Here the guide showed them how the warehouse-sized pools of untreated water was protected from evaporation before funneling down to the magical filtration system and entering the city.

Briony peeled off her flowing over robe, and kicked off her shoes, then dove into the pool, splashing Kody with shockingly cool water.

"I'll leave you to it then," the guide said to Kody, before making his way back to the ladders leading down. Kody glanced at Tristan.

"She does know that's the water we drink, doesn't she?" Tristan asked.

Briony surfaced and spit a mouthful of water at Tristan. "Weren't you listening? It goes through days of magical filtration before entering the city. Loosen up and jump in."

Tristan met Kody's eyes again, and grinned before pulling off his shirt, revealing all the hard work of his blacksmith skills. Kody tried not to be too obvious in watching as he kicked off his shoes and did a cannonball into the pool.

Kody laughed and kicked off her own shoes.

"Come on, turtle girl. I don't have all day," Briony called.

Kody stuck her tongue out at her sister, then plugged her nose and jumped in.

The shock of the cold hit her all at once in a disorienting wave. When her descent slowed, she kicked up to the surface and gasped for air. The pool was deeper than she expected, and she kicked hard to keep her head above water.

Briony linked arms with her and towed Kody away. "It's shallower over here," she called as they passed Tristan, floating peacefully on his back, face serene in the green glow from above.

"Can you do a handstand?" Kody asked her sister as they reached a shallower level.

"Of course. Here, watch," Briony said before trying the trick, her legs pointing straight out of the water as her sopping wet pants clung and pulled her off balance.

"I can do a backflip," Tristan called, coming to join them.

They did tricks and played games like little kids for a while, before crawling out of the pool and sunning themselves in the lightly filtered shade of the leaves.

As Kody rang out her pant legs, willing them to dry faster, her eyes caught on her sister's shoulder, bare in her sleeveless tunic as she lounged on the leaf. Her smokey brown skin glistened in the light, her green swirls winding around her arms and under the edge of her tunic like a vein of emeralds. The light highlighted the line of her forehead, the edge of her cheek and the point of her nose. Delicate features that were not ruined by the green gemstones swirled through her skin, but instead enhanced. Her sister was insanely beautiful, not despite her green Elv features, but because of them.

Kody looked down at her own legs, bare where she'd rolled up her pants, and then at her arms, also glowing in the filtered light. Her own green swirls no longer looked foreign or taboo. Was it possible they made her beautiful, like Briony?

Embarrassed by the direction of her thoughts, Kody unrolled her pants and looked for Tristan. He was on her other side, leaning back on his arms, and watching her with a content smile.

Havu found them a while later and refused Briony's insistence that he take a dip in the pool. Eventually she dried them the rest of the way with magic, and they all started the journey back for family dinner in the willow tree dining room.

When dinner was over, Havu and Briony lingered in the family garden while Tristan escorted Kody back to her room.

Someone stood just inside the entrance of Kody's rooms, examining something, and Kody froze, not sure what to do. Tristan took a step forward, but as the man turned, Kody stopped him, realizing the stranger was the Elv with the nose ring she'd met earlier. When he noticed Kody, he straightened and grinned, showing off his dazzling teeth.

"My love for you is a bud," he said, and Kody blinked, confused. He cupped his hands together close to his chest, as if holding something. "Just now it is tiny and small, but give it time, nurture it well"—He pulled his hands apart as if something inside got bigger—"and it shall bloom into something grand enough to rival any." He turned his arm movements into a flourish and bowed to Kody. Straightening, he tossed a grin at Tristan and wandered out into the night.

"What was that?" Tristan asked.

Kody blinked again, and stepped into her home, afraid of what she'd see.

It was worse than she could have imagined. Nearly every inch of her lovely wood floor had been pried up, the wood stacked in corners and on the furniture, and in the exposed space beneath, the garden section of a hardware store had been planted. There were flowers, shrubs, and trees planted alongside a cactus, several ferns, and climbing vines, and even a few tall sunflowers.

"So, did you order a decorating committee or something?" Tristan asked, stepping up behind Kody.

"Briony said it's—" But she was too embarrassed to continue.

"It's what? Some type of hazing?"

Kody bit the inside of her lip, her cheeks growing hot. "Kind of. It's a courting ritual or something. They do it to show interest, but it's also like a game."

Tristan took a step closer and peered around the room. "I didn't realize you'd made so many friends already."

Kody didn't know what to say. She hadn't realized she'd met so many people during her day with Briony, either.

"Well, good luck with your jungle," Tristan said, before leaving the room.

Kody, with an ache in her chest, looked back at the room. There was what felt like a path on the left, but she wasn't sure it would get her to her bedroom. On the right she could try to jump on the couch, like a kids' game pretending the floor was lava, but then she noticed some floorboards stacked on the couch had nails in them, and that seemed like a bad idea.

"The people have spoken."

Kody jumped, then glared at her sister, who stood leaning against the doorjamb, grinning. "You're the hottest new thing since Caster figured out how to dye hair mauve."

"What does this mean?" Kody asked.

Briony laughed. "It means half the city is interested in you."

"They don't even know me."

"That doesn't always matter."

Kody groaned and dug her fingers into her hair. She didn't enjoy being the center of attention. "Did you get this many?"

"I grew up here. People got to know me over time, so mine were more staggered." She shrugged. "Good luck figuring out who planted them before you tear them up."

Kody's eyes nearly popped out of her head. "Why do I have to do that?"

"Well, you don't want to tear one out from someone you like, do you? Or from someone you don't want to insult. There's a right and a wrong way to tell someone you're not interested."

"So dumping the lot over the balcony isn't an option?" Kody asked.

Briony giggled. "Of course, that's an option. It just sets a bit of a tone, don't you think?"

"What tone?" Kody asked, but Briony had already stepped outside. Kody followed her out. "What tone?!" But Briony only cackled into the night and wished Kody sweet dreams.

Kody covered her face with her hands and took a deep breath before returning to her rooms. At least the plants smelled good. She weaved her way through the foliage and was even more depressed to see her room just as full as the living room. There were flowers and shrubs, and some fern with its leaves all rolled up, sitting under a tree, and even a few mushrooms in the mix. Her bathroom only had a few plants, cattails lining her river, and a few water lilies floating in the pool that she kind of liked. Maybe she would just blindly marry the water lily person for having good taste. Kody groaned and got ready for bed.

She had a hard time getting to sleep in her new forest bedroom. The room felt too full with all the plants, and she could swear something was rustling. Kody didn't feel ready to court some Elv she didn't know. Her breakup with Roger was so recent, she should spend some time on her own. But her mind drifted to Tristan, and then she thought maybe she was ready to start seeing someone, that someone just wasn't an Elv.

After her long talk with Briony about her breakup the night before, Briony had told her that relationships weren't exactly discouraged among the Elv and Hu, but they weren't encouraged either. It was a hard life to live, your spouse growing old and dying while you remained young and nearly unchanged. It had been hard for their father to recover, and it was a path Briony said she didn't envy.

Kody didn't disagree. It didn't sound like an easy path, but she didn't even know if it was an option. She thought Tristan liked her, but was it enough for him to leave his people and live among hers? Was it enough for him to choose her, even knowing he would quickly outgrow her?

She automatically assumed it would be Tristan moving here permanently and not her moving back with him, as if somewhere over the course of the day her mind had been made up, and she knew she was staying forever.

Kody rolled over, trying to find a soft spot in her incredibly plush bed. Something brushed lightly against her exposed ankle and Kody kicked her foot. Stupid Elv must have let a bug in when invading her room.

Something touched her ankle again, more firmly this time. When she went to kick, her body didn't respond.

Chapter Fifteen

Kody's heart pounded at double speed in her chest, and the pressure tightened around her ankle. She tried to kick again, and again her leg wouldn't move. Kody tried to turn, but she couldn't. She tried to pull down her blanket, but her arm wouldn't work. She yelled, but only a muffled moan came out. She couldn't wiggle her toes or blink her eyes, or even swallow. Her whole body, except for her breathing, was paralyzed. Her heart pounded harder.

The pressure at her ankle snapped tight and her leg jerked off the side of the bed all on its own. Her ankle burned where something pulled her, until she fell off the bed in a heap, her face squishing a round mushroom. Thankful Elv beds weren't as high in the air as their houses, Kody tried to see what had a hold of her, but the angle was wrong. Instead, trapped in her own body, she slowly slid across the floor, and over plants of every kind, by her ankle. Her arm caught on the stump of a small tree, but the burning hold on her ankle pulled her past it, scraping up her arm.

Kody wanted to scream, to plead and beg with whatever or whoever was doing this, but her efforts were fruitless. As she was dragged over a particularly pokey bush, Kody gave up hope. She couldn't fight something that prevented her from moving. Was it a spell? Some rope around her ankle planning to pull her off the large branch where her rooms resided, plunging her to her death?

"Kody! Kody, are you okay?" Kody heard Tristan's voice calling for her, and she wanted to sob. A tear of frustration fell from her open eye, and she willed Tristan to find her. "Oh my gods, Kody." He was at her side, moving her head to face him. His eyes widened when he saw her glaring back. She tried to scream with her eyes. Her ankle tugged her out of his grip and her head flopped back to the floor. Tristan scrambled down her body to her leg. She felt his hand on her foot.

"What the hell. Ouch! Let me get something. I need a knife or something."

Tristan left her, and she wanted to scream. She didn't have a knife.

"Help!" Tristan's voice called outside of her apartment. "Someone help! Briony! Guards! Someone come quick!"

She heard footsteps again, and then something breaking, and Kody wished she could turn her head to see. Tristan returned a moment later, and he put one hand on her foot near her ankle.

"Hold still, I've got glass and I'm going to cut it."

Holding still was out of Kody's current skill set, as she continued to be pulled across the floor. The something on her ankle tightened, and Tristan grunted. Another long moment, and the pressure on her ankle loosened.

"Okay, I got it. Are you okay?" Tristan asked. "Shit! It's growing a new one!"

Kody desperately wanted to know what he was talking about, but he grabbed her arm and pulled her in the other direction a few feet. Then he picked her up and threw her over his shoulder.

"Tristan? Kody? What's wrong?" Briony called.

Tristan carried Kody out of her rooms and met Briony at the foot of the stairs leading to her house.

"One of those freakish plants in there attacked her."

"What?" Briony asked. "Roke, go look, please."

Someone moved past Kody.

"What's wrong with her?" Briony asked.

"I don't know. She isn't moving, but her eyes are open."

Tristan set her down, and Briony and Tristan crowded into view. Kody tried screaming with her eyes again.

Briony gasped. "Why isn't she speaking?"

A man in uniform trotted out of Kody's rooms holding a plant by its roots as two more men in uniform came down the path.

"It's a fox's noose," the man said, grimacing.

The guards and Briony gasped.

"What is it?" Tristan asked.

Kody's eyes and the scratches over her body burned.

"Call a healer," Briony ordered. "Bring her to my room quickly." Tristan picked Kody up again, this time holding her against his chest as he ascended the stairs. He laid Kody in Briony's bed and a healer appeared, followed by her father and stepmother moments later. Everyone spoke at once, examining her ankle and the plant that attacked her while the healer placed his hands on Kody's leg and glowed a faint green.

"It's a fox's noose, also known as a preyhold," Briony explained to Tristan. "A carnivorous plant that attacks large mammals resting nearby. It's attracted to the heartbeat. Its vine has small stingers for injecting a paralytic. When it pulls you into its base, it injects other poisons to help break down the prey."

Kody wished she could shut off her ears; this was not information she needed right now. The healer had closed her eyes for her, explaining they would dry out, and Kody was grateful for the relief, but not being able to see her surroundings while also unable to move made her feel vulnerable and anxious.

"Is it permanent?" Tristan asked.

"No," the healer said at last. The glow through her eyelids faded, and she could no longer feel the healer's hands. "The paralysis is temporary and should be gone in a few hours. The plant was not able to inject her before she was separated. She needs rest and should be fine by morning."

Kody's family sighed and muttered their relief.

"Briony," said the deep voice of Havu, just arriving as far as Kody could tell. "What happened, my love? Is everything all right?"

"No, some stupid fool planted a preyhold in Kody's bedroom. She's going to recover, but we need to figure out what dunce did it."

Havu took longer than a moment to respond. "A preyhold? How did she survive the assassination attempt?"

"Assassination, please. It was probably some moron who thought it was pretty," Briony said.

"I found her," Tristan added.

Havu's voice grew deeper. "And what were you doing in the princesses' bed chambers?"

"Havu, stand down," Minda said, her voice sharper than Kody had ever heard it.

"Havu, be kind. Tristan wouldn't do this," Briony said gently.

"So we are to believe the Hu wandered up hundreds of feet just as the princess was being assassinated?" Havu asked.

"It was the god," Tristan said. "Ravid. I had a dream, and he told me he owed me a favor and that I should go check on my—on Kody, then I woke up." No one spoke, and Kody wished someone would open her eyes again. "What? I'm not making it up."

Kody's father spoke next, in a slow, careful voice. "You speak of one of the gods of the Hu. What do you know of these creatures that one should owe you a favor?"

"Nothing, he tricked me into doing something once," Tristan said. "It was a long time ago."

"The Hu and their weak minds allowed those parasites into this world. We don't allow their kind into our lands," Havu bit out.

"Look, it's not like I invited him. I want nothing to do with them either," Tristan said.

"Enough of this. Kody needs to rest. We can argue in the morning," Callum said. "Havu, assign your best guards to this room tonight."

"I'm staying too," Briony added.

"I'll send someone with a bed pallet."

"Thanks, Dad."

The floor creaked, as Kody assumed people shuffled outside. Then someone ran a hand across her forehead. "Rest daughter, you will be protected tonight," her father said.

Things became calm for a short time, and then something or someone rummaged beside her.

"Don't worry, it's just me," Briony said. "I'm going to sleep right here, so anyone has to get past me to get to you." Briony shifted on the floor next to Kody, and eventually was still.

Kody lay there for a long time, unable to let sleep take her, until a slight tingling started in her toes and fingers, and she could wiggle the tip of her pinky. The small action was the reassurance she needed. Relief from the anxiety and fear leaked from the corners of her eyes, and at last, she drifted to sleep.

Chapter Sixteen

The sun cast bright rays of light through the window, and Kody rolled over to bury her face in her pillow. The pillow smelled like Briony and made her smile. Kody jerked awake. Briony sat up on the pallet next to the bed, her sleepy eyes looking over every inch of Kody as the two sat there, silent for a moment.

"How do you feel?" Briony asked.

Kody yawned and fell back on the mattress. "Tired. I can wiggle my toes and close my own eyes, though, so I can't complain too much."

Briony lay back on the pallet and looked up at the ceiling. "Thank you for not dying," she whispered.

"Thank Tristan for that. I was absolutely helpless." Fear from the night before clogged up Kody's throat, and she fell silent.

"We should resume magic training. Tristan is right. It's not the only answer, but it helps."

Kody blinked and covered her face with her hand. "I didn't even think about magic. How stupid am I?"

Briony chuckled. "Give yourself a break. You didn't even know you could do magic a week ago. That's what training is for. It gets you so comfortable with it that you don't have to think in a crisis."

Briony made Kody tea and brought it and a tray of breakfast items with her as she crawled on the bed next to Kody. They ate and talked about nothing, getting crumbs on the quilt and laughing. Kody wasn't excited about going back to her room and wished the peace of the morning could last forever. Tristan stopped in an hour later and joined them, sitting on the floor, and asking Briony about the blacksmiths they'd toured the day before. Both her father and stepmom checked in on her throughout the morning and were relieved to see her totally recovered. Even the scrapes and cuts she'd endured while being dragged through the forest of plants in her bedroom were now healed.

Around lunch Havu came in, bringing a tray of meats, cheeses, and crackers. He glared at Tristan sitting on the floor. "How did you get up here?" he asked.

Tristan acted as if Havu's hostility was normal. "I used the central lifts like usual."

"Who let you through the checkpoint?" he demanded, shaking off Briony's hands as she tried to calm him.

"Oh, I'm not sure," Tristan said disinterestedly as he fiddled with the tea mug by his leg. "All the guards look alike, to be honest."

Kody rolled her eyes, as she'd seen Tristan greeting several by name the day before. Havu also did not seem convinced.

"Havu, let it be. Mom and Dad are perfectly fine with Tristan coming as he wishes. They don't believe any more than I do that he's a threat."

"We'll see," Havu said before storming out.

Briony sighed. "I'm sorry Tristan, he can get a little carried away about security."

"Don't worry about it."

"You don't really think it was an assassination attempt, do you?" Kody asked.

Briony frowned. "I can't see any reason for it. Politically, killing you would do little but cause grief and heartache for our father."

"That's not entirely true," Tristan said.

"What do you mean?"

"Well, if the right people or political party were blamed for her death, at the very least, it could lead to your father setting policies and laws that are biased against that party. At worst, it could lead to a war against whoever led the attack. Then there's the question of who will rule after Callum. If Kody's out of the picture, that position goes straight to you."

Briony rolled her eyes. "My father still carries the potential to live a very long life. There's no reason thoughts of leadership should come into this when he might be in power for centuries more. Besides, if it came to an argument, I would happily give up any claim on the throne to Kody," Briony proclaimed.

"No, thanks." Kody laughed.

Havu stepped back through the bedroom door, his cheeks and the tips of his ears pink.

"Havu, sit," Briony said, pulling the tall Elv to a chair. He looked pissed and shot a deadly glare at Tristan but let Briony guide him. "Let me make you tea and you can tell us if there are any leads of who planted the preyhold."

Tristan stood and stretched out his legs, avoiding Havu's glare. "I should get going."

"See you for dinner?" Kody asked.

"Yeah, sure," he said with a small smile before following Briony out.

Kody felt a little uncomfortable in the room alone with Havu, who didn't speak or shift in his chair, continuing to look at the bedroom door with a tense frown as if waiting to lunge into action. The seconds crept by until Briony returned, sat on his lap, and coaxed information out of him. He had little to tell them. The guards had made a long and exhaustive list of every Elv and Hu who had entered the royal family's private section the day before and had a second list of every plant in Kody's rooms and where it was planted. Guards were now questioning every person on the list. They would look for inconsistencies to help narrow down the suspect pool.

Kody excused herself, feeling like a bit of a third wheel, and refused Briony's offer of an escort back to her rooms. It was a short walk, and Havu had said the guards were being very careful about who they let in.

As she approached her rooms, she feared what she would find inside. She wouldn't feel safe until every plant was out, and she didn't relish the thought of uprooting a hundred plants. She just wanted to bathe the night of fear off her skin and change into something that wasn't pajamas.

Kody opened her door and was not greeted with hordes of plants and torn up floorboards. She took a step further and relief filled her. Not only had the floor been put back, good as new, there wasn't a single living thing inside except for . . . "Tristan?"

Tristan was bent over in the corner of her room, prying up floorboards with an oddly shaped crowbar. He stood and turned, his cheeks quite pink. He picked up a small plant and held it out to her.

"I'm blooming," he said.

"What?" Kody wasn't sure if she should call him a doctor or water him.

"I'm blooming for you. My love, it's a flower." He held up a shrub that definitely wasn't a flower, sticking out of a burlap sack.

"Is that a begonia?" Kody asked.

"Do I really look like I know?"

Kody bit her lips, trying not to laugh. He'd used the L word, and she was feeling giddy. "Where did you find it?"

"It's best if I don't tell you that." He looked so serious saying it, and Kody almost lost it. "Look, I like you, and I wanted to show it by meeting you on your ground with your culture and traditions," Tristan said, offering the begonia.

"Tristan."

"Yeah."

"This isn't my culture," Kody told him.

He looked confused at her words, Kody couldn't help but smile and step forward, the small shrub the only thing between them. "I was raised on Earth," Kody whispered.

Tristan frowned. "Okay. Then how am I supposed to ask you out or tell you I'm all serious about you or whatever?"

"I think you just did."

"Right. So now I should . . ."

"Put down the plant," Kody suggested.

Tristan tossed the begonia in the corner and reached for Kody, who was already there, wrapping her arms around his neck. He kissed her and the world seemed to come to a stop. Nothing else mattered when Tristan had his hands on her.

After many kisses, Tristan pulled away and laughed when Kody tried to pull him back. "I need to tell you something," he said, and Kody stopped, realizing his tone was serious. Serious enough that tea and a soft spot out of each other's reach on the couch were necessary, so it seemed.

"I wanted to tell you why that god owed me a favor, since everyone made such a big deal out of it," Tristan said at last, after his first sip of tea.

"I don't know anything about the gods of this world," Kody cut in.

"Well, I asked someone in town about it, and apparently the Elv have one god, a creator god. The Hu have quite a few, actually. Gods with different roles or things they help with, always battling each other for the favor of a person. Growing up, I never questioned it, it was just another weird thing the Twoshy had that Earth didn't."

"Well, it's not so weird for the Elv not to like the Hu's gods, is it?" Kody asked. "Weren't there hundreds of wars fought on Earth for the same reason?"

Tristan raised his eyebrows. "That's a good point. But it goes further, I think. I've heard people say that the Hu gods aren't really gods, and may or may not actually be from this world. I don't know. I know someone who got the complete story from some dragons, but I wasn't there."

"Wait. Dragons? I thought that was a joke." Kody made flapping motions with her arms.

"Again, I wasn't there. You should ask your dad, actually. The Elv have a longer history with the dragons than the Hu. But anyway, that's not the point. It doesn't matter what the gods are or where they came from. The point is, they like to interfere."

"So more like the Greek gods?" Kody asked.

"Exactly. Only not as much baby making as far as I know," Tristan said, grimacing. "Their goals are to gain followers, people to worship them."

"And how did that equal them owing you a favor?"

Tristan sighed. "It was this one god. There's this other Misplaced who's now queen of Aluna, her name's Elodie."

Kody leaned in, so ready to have the story Tristan had hinted at. Tristan had grown so bleak back in his apartment when these people and places were brought up, and Kody was desperate to finally know why.

"Back when we were all teens, the steward of her country tried to assassinate her. He accused her of treason and orchestrated a manhunt against her."

Tristan sighed and got up, adding more honey to his tea.

"You don't have to tell me," Kody said to be polite, wishing with everything she had he wouldn't take her up on it.

Tristan stirred his tea and sat back down, not looking at Kody. "I was in a bad place. Right before the Twoshy sucked me in I'd just run away from a crappy foster family, and a cop picked me up. I vanished right out of his back seat, still wearing handcuffs."

Kody gasped. "Why'd he cuff you?"

Tristan rolled his eyes. "Wanted to scare me or something. I was sleeping on a bench and trespassing charges probably wouldn't have stuck, but it still could have been bad. He didn't have my name or anything, so the magic actually saved me for once. Once I got the cuffs off, at least." Tristan took several more sips of tea, as if trying to buy time. Kody wanted to grab him and shake the story from him. "It's not an excuse, but I was angry at everyone and everything, and then this god shows up while I'm on guard duty and says I should sell Elodie out. Tell the Steward's men where she's hiding. He even offers me an orb to communicate with them, just in case. I told him off and refused to take it. He said Elodie wouldn't be harmed, and I could talk a reward out of the guards, enough to buy my own forge. I still didn't take it," Tristan said. He turned to Kody and looked her in the eyes. "I didn't take the orb."

Kody nodded. "I believe you."

Tristan fell back against the couch. "It didn't matter. When I went upstairs, it was in my pocket. And then Elodie tried to sneak outside. There we are, a dozen people risking our lives to protect her, and she's trying to sneak out. Elodie had it pretty easy compared to the rest of us Misplaced, and when I saw how entitled she was, thinking she could just spit in everyone's faces and walk out? I snapped. I called the guards and worked out a reward, and they snuck up and caught her."

Tristan went quiet, and Kody waited three long minutes before speaking. She knew it was three minutes because she counted, so as not to appear too eager.

"And?"

"And what?" Tristan asked, the bleak, broody man she'd met back in full force.

"And did she die?"

"Does it matter?"

"Yeah, it matters."

Tristan sighed. "She didn't die. She freed herself and helped take out the steward, and the day was saved."

"And you still feel guilty about it." It wasn't a question.

"Of course, I still feel guilty. I betrayed an ally in their time of need. I didn't even collect the reward money, just fled for the border before my friends realized what I'd done, like a coward."

"How long ago was that?"

Tristan shrugged. "I don't know. Time flows weird between worlds. I would spend a year in the Twoshy, then live the same year again on Earth. I was sixteen when it happened, but I celebrated my eighteenth birthday three times, so who really knows?"

Kody nodded slowly. "So it's safe to say you've been brooding over this for at least a decade. Isn't that enough?"

Tristan frowned and looked at her, his bangs falling into his face. "I haven't been brooding."

"Oh yes, you have. You're brooding right now." She tried to hide her grin.

Tristan frowned harder. "No, I'm not. And I deserve to feel guilty over something I did wrong."

Kody sighed. "Do you regret it?"

"Yes."

"Would you do it again?"

"Absolutely not."

"There. That means you can let it go and forgive yourself."

Tristan frowned harder and looked into his teacup. "It's not enough."

"Maybe you should write her a letter," Kody suggested.

Tristan laughed. "Yeah, I did group therapy, too. Write a letter and set it on fire to release me of all my burdens, right?"

"No, I think you should send it."

Tristan looked at her, confused, as if the thought had never occurred to him before.

"Do you want or need her forgiveness?" Kody asked.

Tristan shook his head. "No."

Kody nodded. "Perfect. Then send the letter. If you wanted her forgiveness, I would tell you not to send it, because that's the wrong reason. You don't need a reply, but telling her you regret it, apologizing with absolutely no strings attached, it might help take the weight off."

Tristan thought about it and nodded. "Maybe I should have listened more in group therapy."

Chapter Seventeen

The next morning, Kody awoke and smiled at the begonia she made Tristan finish planting in the corner before they went to dinner. A lightness swirled in her as she watched the birds flitting outside her window before rising for a cup of tea. The breakfast tray was void of food, but a note was pinned under the teapot. "Please meet me for breakfast next to my pond." It was signed "C."

Her father hadn't said anything the night before about breakfast, but she was delighted he'd thought of her, even if he was forcing the invite by not having a proper breakfast waiting for her. She pulled her clothes on and took the lift down to the atrium tree.

The path to her dad's office was empty this early, and Kody smiled, thinking about her dad getting an early start on the day before anyone was around to bug him. Birds of every color fluttered through the morning air in Callum's wild garden and Kody breathed in the fresh air, anxious yet excited for more alone time with her dad.

She found the pond with ease, the water glittering with colors. Her father wasn't in sight, but she stepped up to the edge of the bank and watched the fish more active in the early morning than they'd been on her first trip.

She heard someone behind her and turned, expecting Callum, but it was Havu in his guard uniform.

"Oh. Good morning, Havu," Kody greeted, but Havu didn't return the gesture. Instead, he reached for her, and Kody shied away, afraid he would try to embrace her. Had she read him so wrong?

When Havu's fingers closed around Kody's throat, she decided she had in fact read him wrong. Kody gasped, but no air rushed back in as Havu's hands tightened around her neck.

Her hands went to his fingers, trying to pry them away, but he was too strong. She tried to kick at him, but Tristan was right, he was well prepared for that line of attack.

Havu dragged her by her neck and slammed her up against the tree lining the pond. Scratching at his arms and exposed hands, she tried to remember the tricks Tristan had shown her, but her eyesight and her mind were growing fuzzy with panic. Havu tightened his grip. Using one hand to pin her against the tree, he leaned forward and played with something at her neck.

"He made this for you, didn't he?" Havu held Kody's bridge pendant up for her to see, but she couldn't respond. "After I strangle you with it, I will hide it in his rooms for them to find. No one will doubt me then."

He wrapped the necklace around his fist, pulling tight as the chain under his hand cut into Kody's neck. She tried to call out, but the cry was stuck in her throat. Her vision wavered, and she closed her eyes. A million thoughts flashed through her mind until she saw Tristan by the river, flying back with the magic she'd created.

But Kody couldn't think well enough to do magic. It was too new, and she was too weak.

The resolve that had gotten Kody through college while working full time and pushed her forward in every plan she ever created flowed into her, and Kody clenched her teeth. She remembered the magic, the bubble of space she'd created, and then she forced it into being.

With a sharp jolt, the necklace clasp broke against her neck as Havu, holding it tight, flew away from her and crumpled against the bench.

Gasping for air, Kody knelt on the grass, forcing breath into her lungs as quickly as her throbbing throat would allow. Fear made Kody look up. Havu's eyes opened, and he moved. Desperation forced Kody to her feet, made her run.

She could hear Havu pounding down the path behind her. She couldn't make it, but she had to. Following the curving path, there was nowhere to break off, nowhere to hide. Havu closed the distance between them. His longer stride giving him an edge and Kody forced more speed into her fading legs. If she could just get to the door, she might not get it open before he was on her, but maybe someone would be inside, someone would hear her.

Rounding the last corner around a tree, she felt his hands snag in the loose fabric at her back and pull. Kody lost her footing and went down. Screaming a hoarse, shrill cry, she kicked and scratched, feeling satisfied when she pulled a grunt from the blond Elv. She'd nearly gotten her thumb into his eye socket when he went suddenly still against her and rolled away. Kody took the opportunity and crawled. Forcing her legs under her, she stood and ran into Callum. His eyes raging, he pulled her close, and she collapsed against him.

"What happened?" he asked in a scary voice.

"He—" Kody started, but her throat seized and she coughed, pulling away from her father and bending in half with the force of the cough. Her father held her up and rubbed her back.

Briony and Tristan stood a few feet away. Tristan ran his eyes over her, looking worried, but Briony's stony gaze only fell on Havu, laying on his back with his arms and knees bent as if frozen in place.

"Briony—" Kody tried, before coughing again.

"Tristan said you weren't in your room," she said, her face cold and her voice harsh. She held up the note Kody had found. "This isn't Dad's writing."

She closed the distance between Kody and her father, and Kody stood, Callum helping to support her weight. Briony placed a gentle hand on Kody's throat. Her soft touch burned. Briony sighed and pulled away. "I'm a terrible healer." She took a long deep breath until her face smoothed out, then she put her hand back on Kody's throat.

A cool light pressure wrapped around Kody's throat, soothing the burn. She tried to speak again, and it came out raspy. "He was waiting by the pond," Kody told them.

"Did he say why?" Callum asked.

Kody shook her head. "Just that he would frame Tristan after I was dead."

Tristan's eyes got big, and they flicked to Havu.

"Well then. We will have to ask him ourselves," Callum said. "Daughter, will you call a guard with suitable magic to assist?"

"I can do it," Briony bit out.

"Yes, my dear. But you shouldn't have to," Callum said kindly.

"I need to do it," Briony said and stepped closer to Havu.

Kody followed, Callum accompanying her, and after a pause, Tristan approached slowly.

"Can't he break your spell?" Kody asked, a little afraid.

"Havu, much as I, cannot influence the ruakh," Callum told her, running a soothing hand down Kody's back.

She should have known that. She should have asked.

The four of them circled Havu's head, and Briony closed her eyes and took a deep breath. Vines grew out of the ground and wound around Havu, circling his body and legs in thick ropes of green. After a moment, movement returned to him, and the vines tightened, pulling his legs straight and his arms tight against his sides.

He growled. "Let me go! This is a misunderstanding." His voice softened, and he turned his head toward Briony. "Love, this isn't how it looks. I did nothing wrong."

Briony's face was blank and expressionless. She reached down and pulled Kody's necklace from between the vines next to him and handed it back to Kody.

Havu growled again and thrashed against his bindings. "It was her! Don't you see? All of this was her doing. Her and the Hu! They are conspiring against you."

"If you do not wish to speak facts, I can call for a guard to bring something that will make you more honest," Callum said lightly.

Havu grimaced but said nothing. Tristan's fingers brushed against Kody's, and she squeezed his hand tight.

"Why?" Briony asked, her voice holding no emotion or inflection.

"For the throne, obviously." He rolled his eyes, and Kody saw Tristan's foot twitch, as if he wanted to kick Havu.

"Did you wish for me to be queen so badly?" Briony asked.

Havu pursed his lips as if he wouldn't answer, but apparently the temptation was too much. "No, you stupid girl. I wanted to be king."

Briony said nothing but rocked back on her feet as if slapped.

"Your family is polluted, while mine remains pure. How can the Elv stand having such disgraces on the throne? I would have fixed everything! I would have built us to be a powerful people who would fight back against the invading plague on our land!"

"I think we've heard enough," Callum said, placing a hand on Briony's back. Vines grew again, once round his neck and then around his face until they filled his mouth like a horse's bridle, preventing any legible words from escaping. Havu yelled, but none of it formed words. Briony raised the vine wrapped cocoon into the air, and the vines snapped free of their roots, the living ends sinking back into the path as Havu hung suspended. They left the garden, an odd parade of sorts, and Callum made Kody sit in a chair while he fetched guards to take Havu away.

Kody tried to catch her sister's cold, blank stare as a healer escorted her back to her rooms, Tristan following. She asked Tristan to stay as the healer gave her something to rest.

Chapter Eighteen

It was just afternoon when Kody awoke to Tristan reading in a chair near her bed. He doted on her for a bit, and brought her tea, and Kody let him. Her throat was as good as new, the swelling completely gone.

"I fixed the clasp," Tristan said, offering back her bridge necklace. "If you still want to wear it. I totally get it if you don't," he said, looking away. Kody sat up and moved her hair out of the way, a clear invitation for him to drape it around her neck. His fingers lingered a little longer than they needed to, and he kissed her forehead. "I'm glad you didn't die."

Kody chuckled and was relieved when it didn't hurt. "Are you just saying that because you would have been convicted of my murder?"

"No." He grinned. "I like the world a little more when you're in it."

Kody smiled and leaned into him, feeling as if a weight had been lifted off her shoulders.

"I need to go check on Briony. Will you wait for me?"

"Always," Tristan said, and let her go when she stood, her legs just a little unsteady.

Kody climbed the stairs to Briony's rooms. She was nervous, and not sure why. When she reached the door, she knocked, and the door opened without a word. Kody stepped in slowly, not wanting to disturb her sister.

The sitting room was empty, and Kody slowly crossed to the bedroom, where a green glow flickered through the doorway.

Briony sat on her bed, watching a small fire in the middle of her room as the last of a chalky white trunk disintegrated into ash. A large gaping hole in the middle of the floorboards and blue star-shaped leaves scattered around the room were all that was left of Havu's tree.

"Are you feeling all right?" Briony asked, her expression still blank, her voice empty.

"Yes, I'm fine."

"Good."

"Are you okay?" Kody asked.

"Yes."

"Do you want to talk about it?"

"No."

Kody nodded before she turned and fled.

She returned to her rooms and told Tristan she wanted to take a shower and relax before dinner. He agreed, kissing her forehead before leaving, and Kody let out a tight breath before sinking down behind the closed door.

Everything was over now. She could feel it in her bones. She'd had a lot of foster families. Some were better at making her feel wanted than others, but it never felt real. Her final foster parents, they were good people, but her staying there had always felt temporary. They cared for her, but when she turned eighteen, she knew it was time to leave.

This magical Elv family had felt more real somehow than all the others ever had, but now it was broken. It felt like the time she was six and lived with a lovely family with a biological daughter Kody's age. The little girl wanted a sister her own age to play with, and the parents wanted to try fostering. Kody was their first.

The first day was lovely, full of tea parties and dress up, and ended with the daughter wanting to play catch with a teddy bear in her bedroom. They threw the bear back and forth a dozen times before Kody threw it too hard and knocked a porcelain doll off the shelf, cracking its face.

The daughter, Kody couldn't even remember her name, screamed and screamed and screamed in Kody's face, long after the parents came in and tried to pull her away. Kody cowered in the corner, her hands over her ears until the mom walked her back to her own bedroom and tucked her in.

She didn't sleep. She knew the moment the doll tumbled from the dresser they would send her back, and when the mom came in the next morning to wake her, Kody was already dressed, packed, and ready to go.

This mirrored that moment. Havu had tried to kill her, and Briony's heart was rightfully broken. Kody didn't have any illusions about how that kind of pain felt, and she didn't blame her sister for rejecting her.

When it was time for dinner, Tristan knocked on Kody's door, and they went to the family garden. She entered the privacy of the willow tree and was pulled into a hug by Minda, who held her tight and asked her how she was. Kody barely felt it.

"I'm fine," she told her stepmother and then her father.

The table was only set for five, and Kody sat between her father and Tristan as they waited for Briony.

"You need not worry," Callum said, interpreting Kody's stillness incorrectly. "Havu will never bother you again."

"What are the punishments for such actions among the Elv?" Tristan asked.

"Isolation and imprisonment, for many years, followed by banishment. He will be sent somewhere he can be watched and can make himself useful."

Tristan nodded. "Rohap does something similar, although imprisonment doesn't last as long for a Hu."

The conversation lulled on the dreadful topic, and a still expressionless Briony entered a few moments later, her hair a little messy, and ash on the edges of her sleeves.

She nodded to everyone present as she sat in the remaining seat.

They ate dinner with little conversation, and Kody only picked at her food, her stomach turning, tight and uncomfortable. The servers replaced the dinner plates with a creamy dessert that no one touched, and Kody took a deep breath.

"I wanted to say something," she blurted out.

"Of course, dear, you can say anything," her father said, placing a hand on her arm. The warmth of it burned against her skin.

"I think I should return to Rohap." Kody looked at her plate, unable to meet anyone's eyes. "I've caused too much chaos here, and I never meant to hurt anyone." She glanced at Briony's stony expression. "I came here looking for a family, not a throne."

Briony's face broke at last, splitting into a sob. "You can have it. I don't need to be queen," Briony cried, a desperate plea in her voice.

"But I don't want it!"

"And that's perfectly acceptable." Kody and Briony turned to look at Callum, sitting calmly in his chair, a small smile on his lips. "I don't plan on going anywhere soon. Kody, my daughter. You are new to our world, so you may not be aware. We have a saying among the Elv, that we have all the time in the world."

"The Hu say that too," Tristan countered.

Callum nodded. "Yes, but for the Elv, it's closer to true. The perk of Elv blood is that we have many lifetimes to accomplish our wishes. I may not retire until one of my great grandchildren decides they want the job."

Kody looked down. "I'm sorry, Briony. I'm so sorry that I came here and ruined things for you."

"Ruined?" Briony sobbed. "Sister, you saved me, and it nearly cost you your life." Briony stood and circled the table, and Kody stood just in time to catch her sister as she hugged her tight. "If it wasn't for you, I would have married that disgusting slug slime, all the while he was trying to marry a throne."

Briony sobbed into Kody's chest and Kody gripped her sister tightly. "I'm so sorry, Briony," Kody said, her own tears falling into her sister's hair.

"I'm sorry too!" Briony wailed. "And my mother was *right*!" Briony cried harder, as if that was the greatest crime of all.

"I never said I *didn't* like him," Minda stage whispered.

"Yes, love. But we all know you didn't," Callum said back.

Kody snorted and Briony half sobbed, half snorted, before pulling back from Kody.

"Aw, I'm so sorry. I almost got you killed and then I snotted up your shirt," Briony said.

Kody laughed, wiping the tears from her own face. "Isn't that what big sisters are for?" Kody asked tentatively.

Briony's face broke into a big, weepy smile. "It is." She hugged Kody again, then pulled back and punched her in the arm really hard.

"Ouch!" Kody cried, pulling back.

"And that's for even considering leaving me," Briony said. "Over what? Some boy? You know I would have just followed you and slept on your doorstep, right? I'm your sister. You can't get rid of me!"

Kody didn't have words to reply, and big fat tears fell from her eyes as she hugged her sister again.

Tristan switched seats with Briony, and the sisters pushed their chairs closer so they could hold hands. It felt strange. Just hours before, Kody had been sure her relationship was as smashed as the porcelain doll, and now it somehow felt unbreakable.

All her life she'd felt like a houseplant in too small a pot.

Stunted and strangled, she was destined for a transient life, moving from windowsill to windowsill, trying to find enough light to live.

But now at last her roots had reached soft ground where they could sink deep and stretch far, grounded and strong. If she was going to be blessed with a long life, she would make the most of it.

"Well, I'm glad that's settled," Minda said before taking a bite of the creamy purple dessert before her. "Oh, this is good."

Kody licked her own spoonful of dessert. It was a fluffy berry flavored mouse, and she quickly took a second scoop.

"And what of you?" Callum asked Tristan. "You who have planted a seed in my daughter's heart? Will you stay, or drag her back to your people, if she is willing to be dragged?"

Kody's cheeks got hot, and Briony squeezed her hand, then shot her a suggestive look when Kody looked her way.

"I would like to stay, if you will have me." Tristan nodded to each, nodding last to Kody, who smiled. "I think I can be of use in your forges."

"We would be happy to have you as long as you wish to call the forest home," Callum told him.

A little "Yay!" shot its way, ping-ponging around Kody's mind. She could keep him!

"I need to return to gather my things and end my commitments." Tristan looked at Kody. "I might be gone a few weeks, but you should stay and spend time with your family."

"You promise to return?" Kody asked.

"I promise." His eyes melted into hers when they connected.

"Briony, you should go with him. You promised that king, didn't you?"

Briony looked up, as if just returning to the conversation. She shook her head. "Maybe in a decade or two." She glanced at Tristan, a small smile lifting the corner of her mouth, gave Kody hope her sister was still in there. "Perhaps I will send you with a basket of elder berry tarts, so the king knows he is not forgotten."

Tristan grinned and bowed in his seat. “I am your messenger to command.”

Briony nodded, a gleam of mischief glinting in her eyes as she squeezed Kody’s hand. “Yes, a few decades, I think, and then we’ll see what that king in his beautiful castle is made of.”

Epilogue

Kody raced across the branch pathway, high above the forest floor, and jumped into the hanging basket, causing it to swing wildly before she slapped the knob and rocketed to the ground. She dashed along more branch paths and down the atrium tree's staircase, taking it two steps at a time. In a moment she was outside, rushing through the garden path toward the river, her yellow and green garments flowing behind her.

Tristan had left for Rohap a month ago, an Elv guide in tow to help him navigate the forest there and back, and Kody was just beginning to think he might never return. That is, until Kody received the message three minutes ago that he had just arrived via the river.

Kody took the winding path through the city to the river at a run, dodging and apologizing to the Elv and Hu she passed until she encountered a small group of Hu, led by the most handsome man she'd ever seen. She flung her arms wide and they collided, him catching her up in his strong arms and squeezing tight.

"Sorry, things took longer to wrap up than I thought," Tristan said. He kissed her cheek and was then abruptly shoved out of the way.

“Hi! I’m Sam, your new best friend,” a pretty girl with jet black hair, porcelain skin, and a friendly grin said.

“Actually, I’m going to be your new best friend,” a girl about a foot shorter with lovely eyes and long box braids said, shoving Sam out of the way. “I’m Kat! You spoke to my brother Thomas before.”

“Are we just gonna pretend like we didn’t ride giant frogs here?”

Kody searched for the man who said it. He was a few inches shorter than her with a light brown complexion and straight black hair cut long on top. An identical man stood next to him, looking reserved while observing his surroundings.

It took her a moment, but she realized they were all speaking English, her ears buzzing with the sudden homesickness of it all.

“Yeah, trying really hard to forget the frogs, Kirk. Please don’t remind me,” a tall man she thought was Thomas said.

“You can always walk back if you prefer.”

“Guys, can we please not embarrass ourselves in front of the Elv?”

“Nah, Elv hospitality is the best. Just relax, babe.”

“How would you know?”

They continued arguing in circles and Kody met Tristan’s eyes as he stood just off to the side, his arms crossed. He looked just as broody as the day she met him, and she reached out a hand. He took it and pulled her close, the broody gloom melting away.

“They were waiting for me at the Snarled Cello when I got back, and insisted on meeting you,” he said, his eyes warming by the moment.

“How did things go?” Kody asked.

Tristan nodded. “Good. I left some equipment at the river down south. Apparently the Elv have rafts for bringing heavy loads upriver.”

“So you packed everything you need?” Kody asked, nervous to even ask.

Tristan pressed a grin against her cheek before kissing the same spot. “If you’re asking if I packed up my whole life and brought it here to move in with you, the answer is yes.”

Kody laughed and wrapped her arms around his neck, unable to keep in her joy. “Good,” she said before kissing him properly.

The story of the Twoshy continues...

Prince Kamron lives a charmed life. Growing up with the knowledge of a family curse set to sabotage any of his life pursuits, he discovered a secret to evading grief. If he never truly wanted anything, he could never lose. Instead of wanting, Kam set his aim to see if he could make things happen, purely for curiosity. Get his stogy governess fired? That was easy. Get the capital of his country moved closer to his best friends house? A little harder, but not a problem. Living without want is easy when you have everything you need.

Unfortunately for our prince, his genius plan finds a massive flaw when he finds someone he adores and begins to imagine a life with her. Follow along on this harrowing tale in Unseen Consequences.

About the Author

Heather Michelle is an emerging author of young adult fantasy. She lives in Acworth, GA with her cats; Fitzwilliam, and Mister Bingley, and a slew of unique roommates.

Growing up, Heather Michelle spent more time living in her imagination than outside of it. Small town life sandwiched between the redwood forests and the Pacific ocean provided a rich scope for the imagination. Before the age of twelve, Heather Michelle was not a reader, but a chance encounter with a rented audiobook launched her into the vast world of the printed word, and she never looked back.

For exclusive content, pronunciation guides, short stories, and a guide to the Twoshy by Kirk, visit our website:

www.authorheathermichelle.com

Instagram: @heathermichely

Tiktok: @AuthorHeatherMichelle

www.ingramcontent.com/pod-product-compliance
Lightning Source LLC
Chambersburg PA
CBHW030531310726
48979CB00010B/1878/J

9781952857119